The
Performance

The

Performance

Claire
Thomas

RIVERHEAD BOOKS · NEW YORK · 2021

RIVERHEAD BOOKS
An imprint of Penguin Random House LLC
penguinrandomhouse.com

First published in Australia and New Zealand by Hachette Australia,
an imprint of Hachette Australia Pty Limited, Sydney, in 2021.
First North American edition published by Riverhead Books, 2021.

Grateful acknowledgment is made for permission to reprint the following:

Excerpt from *Happy Days* copyright © 1961 by Grove Press, Inc. Copyright
renewed © 1989 by Samuel Beckett. Used by permission of Grove/Atlantic, Inc.
Any third party use of this material, outside of this publication, is prohibited.

Excerpt from *One Mole Digging a Hole* first published in 2008 by Pan Macmillan.
Reproduced by permission of Macmillan Publishers International Limited.
Copyright © 2008 by Julia Donaldson.

"Tristes Tropiques" from *White Girls* by Hilton Als. Copyright © 2014 by
Hilton Als. Used by permission of The Wylie Agency (UK) Limited.

Library of Congress Cataloging-in-Publication Data
Names: Thomas, Claire, 1975– author.
Title: The performance / Claire Thomas.
Description: New York : Riverhead Books, 2021.
Identifiers: LCCN 2020045747 (print) | LCCN 2020045746 (ebook) |
ISBN 9780593329160 (hardcover) | ISBN 9780593329184 (ebook)
Classification: LCC PR9619.4.T4755 (print) |
LCC PR9619.4.T4755 P47 2021 (ebook) | DDC 823/.92—dc23
LC record available at https://lccn.loc.gov/2020045747
LC ebook record available at https://lccn.loc.gov/2020045746

Printed in the United States of America
1   3   5   7   9   10   8   6   4   2

Book design by Alexis Farabaugh

Dedicated to Katie Ridsdale

and Annabelle Roxon,

the best two of our three

I can't write one complete sentence about her
because she was her own complete sentence, and
her sentence about herself was better than anyone
else's because she uttered it sort of without thinking
while thinking too much, I can't tell you how
unusual that is in a world where, nowadays, no
one leaves the house without some kind of script.

HILTON ALS, *WHITE GIRLS*

How she enjoyed it! How she loved sitting here,
watching it all! It was like a play. It was exactly like
a play. Who could believe the sky at the back wasn't
painted?

KATHERINE MANSFIELD, *MISS BRILL*

The

Performance

One

Margot is shuffling in a balletic first position along the strip of carpet between the legs of the already-seated people in the theater and the chair backs of the row in front. She is almost late, and only some of the seated legs are shifting sideways to enable her to pass.

Excuse me, Margot says to no one in particular. Excuse me.

She is holding her handbag in front of her, moving it carefully over the row of heads. She is determined not to bump anyone with her bag or her body as she watches her feet in her sandals on the carpet, step step stepping.

As she reaches the center of the row, she looks up to see a young man in the seat next to hers. He stands, nodding his head, all chivalrous and patient.

Thank you, she says, squeezing past him. That's very kind.

Margot sits down and drops her bag onto her lap.

The young man also sits. He presses his forearm on the red velvet armrest between them. His flesh spreads out along the length of the armrest, his fingers hanging down toward the floor.

Margot considers asserting her own claim with her own presumptuous arm, but she doesn't want to touch him. His skin is covered in tattoos and pale ginger hairs. He has goose-bumps from the air conditioning. A parrot is inked onto his arm. Primary colors and a neat, sharp beak. Is he thinking of pirates, perhaps?

You're not usually here on a Friday evening, Margot says.

He frowns at her—an arrow between his eyes.

I'm a subscriber, she explains. You get to know the people around you. She didn't mean to sound territorial. He looks annoyed.

But he replies. A whole sentence. We're doing a bit of Beckett at uni.

Beckett, says Margot. I didn't know that's what we were seeing until I got here. Just grabbed my ticket and fled. I was worried about being late. The traffic is always absolutely dire in the heat, don't you find? People seem to drive very strangely in the heat. And that smoke haze. I thought my windows were dirty for much of the drive until I realized it was just the smoke haze.

I got the tram, the young man says. No air con. That was absolutely dire.

I see, says Margot, turning her face forward. She has an expensive, unobstructed view of the stage.

Margot coughs, more loudly than she would like. She clears her throat.

She is conscious of her bare arms in her shift dress. Her bare legs and sandals. Her bare toenails, unpainted. Her father, many years ago when he was still alive and she wasn't old, told her she shouldn't expose her elbows if she could help it. Wrinkly elbows are aging on a woman, he said. And for decades, Margot wore sleeves. More recently, they've been useful with the bruises. But this summer—this unusually oppressive, stinking season—she decided she was tired of sleeves. She was sick of the cling and the pull. When it is hot, she will have bare arms. And it's been very hot today—still forty degrees at 7 p.m.

The false cold of the theater makes it hard to imagine the heavy wind outside in the real world, the ash air pressing onto the city from the nearby hills where bushfires are taking hold.

Margot loosens her wristwatch from her cooled skin and slides its face back and forth around her arm. Her legs are stretched straight with her ankles crossed beneath the chair in front.

The house lights lower.

The auditorium feels hopeful in the darkness.

Margot coughs again.

The young man beside her fidgets. She knows he is annoyed by her coughs, the jolt of them cutting through the tenuous quiet of the waiting theater.

But then a bell rings! It is harsh and institutional.

The play has started.

The buzz seems to be coming from all around. The audience shudders as people adjust to the shock, rearranging their limbs.

The buzz goes on—so loud—and stops.

Begins again! Stops.

Blazing light.

A woman is buried waist deep in a hill of parched grass. It stretches out around her in a curve of muted green, merging into the flat floor of the stage.

The woman's torso is busy above the grass. She is waking from sleep. Her bosom heaves in a teal ball-gown bodice. She is wearing a pearl choker, and her hair is nonchalant and piled high.

Her face smiles. Smiles a lot. A strange lot, given her situation.

Perhaps her lower half is naked inside the mound. Perhaps she is wearing leggings or an itchy tulle skirt.

The woman is speaking a hurried prayer, her palms together, head bowed. *World without end Amen.*

The light on her is bright.

The light shining on the woman's hair makes a pale patch on her crown as Margot looks down.

The woman presses her hairstyle with her hands. The woman's fingers are washed white by the harsh light.

She leans toward a black bag waiting on the slope of the grass. She pulls it close, opens it wide, rummages through its contents. Her rummaging is mannered. It has intention.

Margot looks down at her own lap. Her own handbag is there in the dark and Margot's fingers are folded over its clasp.

Margot's throat tickles. She tries to suppress a cough, and her mouth splutters open. This is no good. It must be the air conditioning, its sudden dry chill after the heat of the world outside. Margot hasn't coughed all day. Not at home. Not in her office. Not even in the two-hour meeting with the dean that she has been dreading for much of her career.

The question of retirement uttered out loud.

She was staunchly dignified. Reasonable. When she started to extract herself from the dean—I mustn't be late for the theater!—they both made a brief show of collegiality. She noticed a glossy museum catalog on his desk—Matisse or Chagall, something luminous—and asked him about his recent holiday in southern France. He asked her about her newish granddaughter, and made a cloying comment about her nappy-changing skills.

Margot was still attempting to laugh at the joke as she walked from his office into the colored light of the corridor lined with stained glass.

Getting out of her car park was difficult. There was an evening graduation ceremony, and car after car was arriving at a time when Margot could usually swing her Audi up the empty concrete ramps to ground level. She almost had a head-on collision with an SUV between levels three and two, brakes screeching, its driver laughing with a woman in the passenger seat who was cradling a floral bouquet so large that it was visible through the windscreen.

Both the driver and the passenger mouthed apologies to Margot before the driver swerved his vehicle back to the correct side.

Margot's heart was racing. She did not swear at the SUV although that would not have been unprecedented. She sat with her hands on the steering wheel and waited for the ramp to clear.

Since she left campus, Margot has not (as her dearly departed mother used to say) had time to bloody scratch herself. She's certainly not had time to consider the ramifications of the dean's suggestion. He told her, smiling and shaking her hand, that it'd be terrific to touch base again early next week.

Early next week? Touch base? What does that actually mean?

Is there a connotation that their next meeting would be a return to home base, as though the dean's office is a benign meeting place from which they all—academics and administrators alike—satellite out toward their individuated endeavors on campus?

Or is it the specific conversation between them that is progressing around bases?

First base—the initial suggestion.

Second base—the next meeting.

Third base—more details and planning.

Home base—when she leaves for good?

Whatever the jargon that is currently favored, Margot understands the implication and Margot cannot believe it.

The woman on stage is brushing her teeth. Toothpaste froths as she vigorously changes the angle of her hand. Margot despises witnessing this particular bodily behavior. She is unsure whether it is a behavior that warrants being performed on stage. It is possibly intended to repulse.

Just this morning Margot scolded John for brushing his teeth before she left the bathroom. His entire process infuriates her. The amount of paste he uses. The state of the bristles on his brush. The height at which he spits. The velocity at which he spits. The length of time between spits. The final sloppy slurp of water. The way he grabs the hand towel—not his own bath towel—and drags it across his mouth so that later she finds dried toothpaste encrusted into the fabric.

They have been married for over forty years. It would help, it would help just a little, if he could wait until she left the bathroom. And today, of all days. He should have known she'd be tense.

Margot had scolded John without hesitation. It was only later, when she was driving to work, that her stomach clenched with the truth. She had to be more careful now. She had to be much more careful.

Hoo-oo! The woman on stage is trying to get the attention of an invisible man. *Poor Willie.*

Margot had forgotten about him. Margot saw an amateur production of this play when she was pregnant with Adam, and she remembered the woman in the mound, and the light. Margot mainly remembered the light.

But, of course, there is also the man. The absent and useless male. *No zest—for anything—no interest—in life.*

The woman's genitals are inaccessible. Perhaps that's why he's ignoring her. He can't get to his once-preferred orifice. Or perhaps that should be the plural, orifices, if he's a demanding sort.

He also seems to have a talent for sleep. *Sleep for ever— marvelous gift.*

The lucky bastard. What Margot would give to be able to sleep for hours without drinking for hours first. These days she cannot fall asleep entirely sober.

Would John remember the man in the play? Would John remember going to the theater at all that night? It was—how long ago? It was forty-two, forty-three years ago. Yes. Adam is forty-two now. Will Margot ever be unshocked by the fact of herself as the mother of a middle-aged man?

She tries to remember the night she saw this play with John at that small studio theater down the side street in the south of the city. She tries to concentrate on retrieving everything she can about that one night, bringing the details forward as though her mind is an analog filing drawer. She visualizes a series of white index cards moving toward her.

This deliberate remembering is a new thing for Margot. A new practice. Or a new praxis, as certain academics in her department would say. Margot refuses to be patronized by sudoku puzzles or the cryptic crossword—lifting a pen toward one of those activities announces you as a gullible geriatric— and she has instead embarked on this careful consideration of her past. She made the mistake recently of telling an old friend about it. That's very Proustian, Professor, her friend mocked.

Margot knew the director; that's why they went to see the

play all those years ago. He was a pretentious private schoolboy who gave himself a pretentious private schoolboy nickname during the final year of their arts degree. Was it Monty? Jonty? Rossco? Xander? It was Rossco. His name was Ross and he added the -co like he was christening a stallion or a yacht.

Rotten Rossco! Yes! He had quite the reputation. He'd propositioned Margot several times when they were partnered up for a French oral exam during their honors year. She was already dating John, which helped a great deal, as Rotten Rossco was the type who'd only back off if he thought a woman belonged to another man. Absolute charmer. Still, Margot and Ross stayed in touch after graduation. She pitied him—he was very short, maybe that was why, and there was some story about a dead sibling that gave him an air of tragedy—so she dragged John to that small studio theater down the side street to support Ross's burgeoning directing career.

The seats were very uncomfortable. John took off his leather jacket, bundled it up in a ball, and arranged it behind Margot's back to give her pregnant body some extra lumbar support. It hadn't helped. But she was pleased with her new husband's concern for her comfort.

Margot was married to John for only six weeks when she fell pregnant. She was completely peeved. She'd thought it was going to take months, perhaps years, to conceive a child. She'd never had a scare with her previous boyfriends, and they'd only relied on her monthly cycle or pulling out before the climax. It was remarkable she hadn't already been afflicted with something—if not a baby, then at least an infection. During her twenties, she'd accompanied a couple of friends to the new abortion clinic in the old white mansion near the city gardens. But Margot herself never had to confront any consequences of having sex. Not so much as a shaming itch. That luck had given her a false sense of invincibility and a false sense of infertility.

To get pregnant so soon after marriage, that conventional happy consequence, struck her as a perverse sort of bodily betrayal. Perhaps she should have been on the pill, to be sure, but she couldn't stand what it did to her bust and her personality— enlarged them both, in ways that were uncomfortable and difficult to manage.

They'd recently returned to Melbourne from Cambridge. Margot was triumphant with a new doctorate and a job at her alma mater. John was about to begin his residency at the city's leading research hospital. That night at the small studio theater down the side street, she was five months pregnant and only just starting to accept her fate.

Before the play, standing on the footpath in the warm autumn dusk, they drank shiraz out of glass tumblers—a fashionable bohemian receptacle, cheap to buy in bulk—and Margot spilled some wine on her baby bump. She watched the red liquid, like blood, like drool, trailing down her floral tunic.

Rotten Rossco shouted something appalling at her as he walked through the waiting audience—Margot has a bun in the oven! Look at that cook!—and John took a step closer to his wife, from pride or protectiveness or some other masculine impulse she could not discern, not then, not now.

The woman on stage is still talking, still smiling. *Mustn't complain.*

Her smile is a gummy grimace. She is adjusting her spectacles, peering through them to examine her toothbrush. She takes them on and off her face, breathes on the lenses and polishes them with a handkerchief. The spectacles do not seem to be helping her read whatever it is she is trying to read on the toothbrush. *Genuine . . . pure . . . what?*

What would Adam make of those glasses if he were here? Adam would certainly have an opinion. Her confident optometrist son. He would recognize the make and model of the frame. He would tut-tut at the woman's unhygienic approach to cleaning the lenses. He would diagnose the woman's optical impairment, or he would assess the extent to which the actress is plausibly displaying an optical impairment. He'd pontificate about it all during intermission. He'd talk at Margot while she sipped champagne. He'd forget his mother was a literature professor with a solid grasp on a damn metaphor, a woman who could far better explain the pertinence in the play of the inadequate set of spectacles. Oh, it'd be excruciating.

Adam, such a darling little boy, has turned into something quite un-darling in recent times. She's not sure why it has happened.

Maybe he suspects what's going on between his parents and

blames her. Blame the woman. Blame the mother. That's the way it goes, isn't it?

For all his visual prowess, Adam cannot see his hero father with any acuity. As a teenager, Adam latched on to John as a human template, replicating his passions and ways of being. There were the usual clichés—shared football team, shared TV shows—but it also extended to preferences for certain foods, weather, conversational style, clothes. Margot occasionally thought it was cute—her tall son and his father, both wearing navy-blue button-down shirts and chinos, watching the rain and sharing antipasto on the deck, competing to make each other laugh, to better each pun—but she also worried that Adam lacked imagination when it came to forming his character, as though it had never occurred to him that there were myriad ways to live a life. Watching Adam, it would seem that one just had to get older and become one's father. When Adam chose to study optometry—John was an eye surgeon—Margot finally accepted that her son was unlikely to ever surprise her.

She accepted she was the outlier in the domestic trio. She accepted she was the secondary parent. And she accepted the odd freedom that was granted to her with that status. It certainly helped her career.

But Adam's ambivalence toward his mother has sharpened into something harsher. He is endlessly disappointed in Margot. She is forever being politely censured. She throws away her garbage incorrectly. She shops in the wrong shops. She spends too much money at the hairdresser. She buys the wrong food.

She likes the wrong people on television. She gives his baby the wrong sort of gifts. She manages John incorrectly. It wearies her.

She wishes she were more lovable, somehow. She wishes he could just give her a hug and love her.

Perhaps one day he'll get past all the judging.

The woman on stage has put aside her toothbrush and spectacles. *Old things. Old eyes.*

Margot shifts in her chair and crosses her old legs.

She can just make out the shape of her legs in the dark. She is pleased she hasn't lost her ankles, that they haven't thickened with age. Thin ankles are a high-quality feature for the young and old. Combined with shapely calves and slim knees, her legs were finely turned, as John used to say. Like a spindle. As though she'd been whizzed around and molded by chisels.

The tickle in her throat is back. It's a very determined tickle.

Margot coughs again.

The young man beside her fidgets. He continues to colonize the armrest with his flesh. He can have it. Little shit. With his parrot and his tram and his uni.

She could tell him a thing or two about universities. Perhaps the young man is a student at Margot's? He certainly has the requisite sense of entitlement. But he hasn't taken her subjects, she is sure of that.

At the start of each new semester when she stands in front of her undergraduates—first-year students for Captivity and Consciousness: Introduction to Nineteenth-Century Literature; third years for Eliot, James, Woolf (that one is invariably nicknamed George, Henry, Ginny after the initial few weeks)—she feels a blast of feeling go through her body like a minor fever. Part adrenaline, part affection, part sheer joy at the hope she feels for the whole enterprise. Another room full of young people who want to talk about books. Who want to think about books.

How Margot loves her students. She loves their nodding heads, their wry smiles, their awkward cool. And she remembers their faces for years. Lately, after continued requests from other lecturers, the admin staff has provided class lists with headshots of every student. Margot does not need those photographs. She has more than once mentioned to her colleagues that she does not need those photographs.

The young man seated beside her is not one of hers, she is certain. Perhaps he is a theater scholar or an acting student at a regional institution. Or—god help us all—perhaps they teach Beckett in creative writing courses now.

Margot coughs again.

Is it not only the young man beside her who is irritated?

Is the very small woman on the other side of Margot also shifting her body in an indication of annoyance?

And the one diagonally in front, a couple of seats closer to the aisle? Margot watches that woman's profile watching the stage. She has long flared nostrils, a witchy chin, and white hair twisted up and held with a black butterfly clip.

Margot coughs again and the woman's head snaps around toward the sound. They make eye contact.

The woman's head snaps back toward the stage and she sighs audibly, performing her displeasure, as if Margot's minor discomfort is her personal affliction.

Now Margot remembers she has some Fisherman's Friend in her handbag.

She opens the clasp and reaches inside. She feels her theater ticket and a pen and a few old shredded tissues. She finds the packet. It has a handy little resealable seal along one length. She slides open the seal and gets out a lozenge. She pops it into her mouth and it makes a clattering noise against her teeth. Margot considers sucking loudly on the lolly, rolling it around her tongue, banging it against her teeth over and over, as a kind of rebellion. She does not do this. Instead, she holds the lozenge still, her tongue pushing it hard against her palate as it dissolves, its juice making its way down her throat, its taste fresh and medicinal. It's doing the trick.

Margot is relieved and concentrates on the woman in the grass.

The woman is kissing a revolver! Good grief! That was unexpected!

The kissing is furtive and fast.

Margot smiles. God knows, she could do with one of those. A revolver. To kiss. And to kill.

She could pop a neat firearm under her pillow. A hard shape that would push into her head and then her dreams, a protective pressure to counter the man-shaped shape beside her in the bed.

Would she keep such a firearm secret? Or would it be a more

effective deterrent if it were known? You hit me again, I'll shoot you—that sort of thing. But what if he found it first? What if he liked the idea of adding actual weapons to his arsenal for wounding? What if he decided his huge hands balled into fists were no longer enough?

But, Margot, Margot, you are forgetting—none of it is decided, at all. He does not decide any of it. The doctors have all been very conclusive about that. He is not to blame.

Oh. Fuck. Off. Doctors. Fuck right off.

The woman on stage has returned her revolver to her black bag. She is holding a frosted-glass bottle of medicine that contains only a small amount of red liquid. Even from upstairs in the theater, Margot can see that it is a stylized old bottle of medicine, like something lined up on a shelf in the apothecary's shop in a replica colonial village. It has a peeling white label.

Before and after meals. Instantaneous improvement.

The woman unscrews the top and takes a swig, throwing her head back more than necessary to swallow the liquid. She tosses the empty bottle over her shoulder.

A quick smash is audible. And a soft manly groan.

Margot thinks that drinking the medicine is the most sensible thing the woman in the grass mound has done since she woke up for yet another day.

Now the woman is applying lipstick, peering at herself in a compact mirror. The light is ruthless.

The woman smiles. Her smile is sad and faintly desperate.

Margot doesn't much like the woman in the grass.

Then the man crawls out.

A trickle of blood is progressing down his bald pate. An injury from the flung medicine bottle, perhaps?

Margot smiles and crosses her legs.

Two

Summer has once again missed the beginning of the play. Whether she gets to watch it depends on where she's stationed each night. If she's on Stairs, she's already inside the auditorium, so there's a greater chance of getting into one of the two reserved seats in the back row on the aisle. When she's on Door, it's less likely she will sit down at all, given her main task is handling the latecomers in the foyer.

Tonight, she's on Door, and because of the heat and the fires, there were several latecomers.

She stood in the carpeted foyer as the group gathered. One hot-and-bothered person after another, hurrying up the stairs from the car park, their faces scrunched against the air conditioning, disappointed.

Summer greeted them, and explained that the play had started and the next entry point was approximately ten minutes into the first act. She gave a variation on the same speech nine times. She stood waiting with the ticket scanner as each person fumbled in bags or pockets for their phone or the paper ticket they'd diligently printed out.

There was one man who had sodden sweat patches blooming from his armpits and around his chest and near his back collar and over his navel. So many darkened sections of fabric that his green shirt appeared tie-dyed, like something Summer's mother might have worn when she was a child.

He pulled his ticket from his chest pocket and handed it to Summer with an extended sigh. The smell that came out of his mouth was a putrid dead-rodent breeze. She beeped her scanner over the damp piece of paper and gave it back to the man, holding her breath, determined not to breathe him in.

At the ten-minute mark, Summer walks to the heavy black door and listens for her cue.

The sound of breaking glass.

And she opens the door.

The latecomers walk through in an obedient single file. Another usher greets them in the dark, miming the next set of instructions.

Summer keeps the door ajar, and follows the people inside.

She settles into the aisle seat just as a man creeps out on stage, his face divided by a bright line of oxygen-rich blood. It's Willie.

Hello, Willie. It's nice to see you again.

This is the third time she will watch the play but she has not yet caught its beginning. She hopes she will see it before the season ends. As far as Summer is concerned, the play starts with Willie. Willie and the wonky hat he is shoving onto his bleeding head.

Winnie, the woman, is worried about the sun. She is talking as though the man has crawled into a giant oven, that the rays from above are going to cook his flesh, when actually it is she who is stuck in that mound of pale earth, immobile and exposed, like a cut spud on a baking tray.

Summer thinks of her mum. An auburn-haired, green-eyed white woman who grew up in the ozone hole era. The ozone hole had a dual effect on her mum—it made her a vigilante about sun protection, forever chasing her darker-skinned daughter around with a tube of zinc cream in one hand and a floppy floral hat in the other, and it also made her optimistic about the state of the earth because to some extent she believed that environmental catastrophe could be stalled by changing your aerosols to pump sprays.

Summer thinks her mum needs to adjust her perception of risk.

Summer is unlikely to ever get sunburned. Her skin attracts the threat of racism, not the threat of blisters and peelings. Growing up, people often asked if Summer was adopted, and her mum was either defensive about it (She's all mine, I assure you) or a bit embarrassing (I pushed her out, I promise).

When Summer had to take a family photo to school, it was just the pair of them, her mum's pink arm over Summer's brown shoulders, enveloping her.

You two look like one of those adorable Benetton ads, a teacher said when he saw the photo.

Summer didn't want to look like a Benetton ad, whatever the hell that was. She wanted her family photo to be like everyone else's, with a group of matching people in it, or at least an adult male to make sense of the mismatch between mother and daughter.

Summer doesn't share her mum's faith in neat solutions for the planet. Summer is forever anxious about the earth and its creatures and its air and its oceans and its dirt.

She is anxious about its terrifying seams that shift at a glacial pace and then suddenly rip apart. She is anxious about its creeping heat, its melting ice, its consuming waters and fires.

Tear-inducing anxious. Nightmare-inducing anxious.

Just last night, Summer had a drowning dream. She understood herself to be a fish in a glass globe bowl, and she was suddenly picked up and thrown in a violent surge down a toilet. There was a thick shit slurry that gushed over her, filled her gills, and stopped her breath. She woke up with the word landslide looping through her head.

landslide

landslide   landslide

landslide

There are often words looping through her head. She is trying to learn how to grab the loop or tie it up or just watch it roll away.

Summer wraps her arms around herself in the theater's dark.

On stage, Winnie is holding her hat aloft.

The hat is a small dome of slick black feathers reminiscent of a dead seabird washed up on a shoreline after an oil spill. Shiny black slime in the sunlight, clumping itself through plumage.

Winnie keeps lifting the hat up and down above her head, like she might be going to put it on, like she's in *A Chorus Line*. This oily bird body bouncing in the light.

Finally she settles the hat on her head, and now she is talking about her first kiss. She reels off a tangle of images.

Within a toolshed . . . the piles of pots . . . shadows deepening among the rafters.

And Summer's body stiffens with a memory. A workshop space. A corkboard on a brick wall above a long bench laden with hardware. The corkboard evenly perforated with holes and covered with dinky outlines of tools as though each one was a body removed from a crime scene, its strange handles and parts marked out like limbs on sinister angles. The floor is concrete and dotted with dark oil stains where dripping cars were recently parked. Summer is lying on a lilo with her friend Mandy. There is a brown garage door on a huge hinge shut closed to the driveway and the sunshine. There is a plain timber door shut closed to the stairway up to the kitchen. A lawnmower's catcher is overflowing in one corner and the air smells of newly cut grass.

Mandy's family are keen campers and earlier the girls inflated the double mattress with the family pump, playing families, playing mummies and daddies, playing house. Summer is Mummy and Mandy is Daddy and they are in bed because that is what mummies and daddies do. They are covered by a tartan picnic rug, the waterproof sticky side down, woolly scratchy side up. Their shorts and T-shirts are in a pile on the concrete floor. They are hugging very tightly and kissing each other's faces. Mandy has big teeth and chapped lips that taste like a Barney Banana. Summer's ponytail bobble is pressing into her head but she doesn't pull it out.

I love you, says Summer. I love you too, says Mandy.

Summer is nine years old.

Summer will have to rethink the history she's previously detailed to a few interested lovers. Her first kiss was not with Elijah Woodside at the year eight dance, sitting in the seats of the darkened school hall with the vinyl armrest between them and OutKast cranking from the tannoy. Sorry, Elijah, you weren't it at all. It was Mandy Mandy Mandy! On the lilo lilo lilo!

Summer can't wait to tell April about it. Fuck, she might even buy her a Barney Banana and let its sugary yellow melt in drips all over the both of them.

Summer smiles now, her arms suddenly covered in goosebumps. Her neck, her thighs.

Summer first walked into April's workplace with a botanical drawing she wanted tattooed on her leg. April was cool as fuck and a little bit famous with an Insta following Summer had no idea about. April grinned at Summer, threw her drawing in the bin, and did a new sketch, flicking a black Sharpie like a chef with a blade. They agreed on the design and the schedule.

April became intimately acquainted with Summer's thighs

over a series of visits to complete the piece. At the final appointment, April was direct about her desire to stay put —right where she was.

My happiness here is very unprofessional, April said, before pulling off her gloves and crawling up to Summer's face to kiss her hard.

When they had sex, Summer's right thigh was still covered in plastic wrap and she held her legs gingerly apart as April very successfully accessed the rest of her.

And that was it for them both. April's fans had to relinquish their hopes. And Summer's hipster boys too.

The poor boys, said April. The poor fans, said Summer.

That was almost two years ago now, with no sign of things waning. Last night they talked in detail about a forest-bathing business they could run when they were old ladies (once April was over tattoos and the thing that would come after tattoos; once Summer had become and then grown tired of being a successful actor). They would wear long hemp skirts and guide frazzled city dwellers toward the most majestic trees in the bush. Their wise wrinkled fingers would be adept at caressing bark and tickling ferns. Their faces would be restful, mutually adoring, and quick to laugh.

Summer's eyes pop open. How could she forget about the fires? How could she let herself think about anything else?

She sits up in her chair and takes a professional look around the audience. There is little movement among the people in the theater and only an occasional cough interrupts the sound of the voice on stage. Everyone seems engrossed. The performance is working on them. Perhaps they are immune to what is going on outside this cold bubble of culture. Maybe they already felt safe in their city or their suburbs, buffered from the threat of the distant, unpredictable flames.

Summer was at home cleaning the kitchen and listening to the radio when the first news came out about the fires. (Her burgundy shirt with the arts center logo was ironed and waiting on the bed, ready for her shift.) It wasn't a surprise that there were some flare-ups. It was the third day of extreme heat, after a spring with little rain, inside a long-term drought. A Total Fire Ban had been declared for all regions across the state. The experts on the radio were calmly no-nonsense as they chatted with broadcasters struggling to pronounce the names of obscure rural towns. There were voices from the Bureau of Meteorology, the Country Fire Authority, the Metropolitan Fire Brigade, traffic management authorities, various local police brigades, a helicopter pilot. There was the climate scientist offering the big picture. There was the director of a childcare center in the foot-hills with the smaller story. She explained the center's heightened fire danger policy, how they shut and notify families ahead of time, for the benefit of everyone in the community. Summer knew that April had attended that very kindergarten. She had pointed it out to Summer the first time they'd visited April's parents, who still lived in the family home on the mountain.

April was proud to show off the place where she'd grown—the unmade streets, the tremendous trees, the warm, full house with its 1980s cathedral-ceiling extension. Summer thinks of the steep driveway up to the front of the house, and April's mum and dad standing waving at the top of it with Woolf the rescue mongrel panting at their feet, a vision of familial perfection. April was skillful with the winding roads and the perilous driveway— I'm a mountain kid, Sum. My vehicle can handle these curves.

Each time they visited her family home, Summer would watch April grow expansive and relaxed. They'd go for long walks and zoom like crazy children through forest paths, dodging fallen logs and deep sections of crunchy undergrowth. They'd chop wood for the open fire, making wild sound effects that made them feel really butch. They'd pick lurid pink blossoms or huge autumnal branches, according to the season, and bring back armfuls that covered the whole backseat of their car. A couple of months ago, they helped April's dad clear out the gutters. Woolf barked up at them from the foot of the ladder and Summer threw down some leaf litter onto her round brown nose.

April was at work earlier today but then she messaged Summer to tell her she was worried about the fires, that she'd canceled her last clients for the afternoon and was heading home.

Summer waited on their front porch, standing up and sitting down, standing up and sitting down on the bluestone step next to their row of potted succulents. The city was already full of bushfire haze, and when April got home, Summer could smell the smoke in her hair.

April had been in touch with her parents all afternoon. They weren't leaving their house. They were busy preparing to fight any fire. They'd defended the house once each decade since they'd lived on the mountain and they were confident they could do it again. Just before April pulled the plug on her day, she'd received a message stating that another fire had started in the foothills.

The wind is favorable, April explained. That's the thing. Mum said the wind is okay and the blaze is almost contained.

So Summer packed her work uniform, said goodbye to April, and rode to the arts center. Her phone pinged in her pocket several times as she powered along the bike path. The route was darker than normal as she rode its familiar bends, a fiery gloom blocking the sun from mid-afternoon. It was too hot to be cycling, and when Summer arrived at work, she was drenched and thirsty.

She parked her bike and went through the stage door to the staff locker room. The air conditioning had sucked the moisture off her skin by the time she'd taken off her backpack and pulled out her phone.

She called April, who didn't answer. Summer had to get ready. She was never late and she was almost late tonight, trying April one last time before throwing her mobile into her locker and closing the door.

The ushers are forbidden from having their phones on them during a shift but Summer often forgets about the rule. She feels the pocket of her trousers now but April isn't there.

On stage, Winnie is still buried in the hill of parched grass in the bright, white light. She is still gesturing. Still speaking.

Wait for the day to come . . . the happy day to come when flesh melts at so many degrees.

Summer's eyes fill with tears. Fuck. These words. This play.

Summer hasn't noticed that line before, but here it is now, barging into her consciousness like an omen or a prophecy, like something she once would have described as deep and meaning-ful. D&M.

The words. Summer is hungry for the words. At times during the play, she closes her eyes and doesn't watch the stage. She just listens to Winnie's voice and her words. Their rhythms. Their echoes. She thinks she has never encountered a play that might mean so much. She thinks theater is often so literal, full of punchy banter about politics and real life, but she longs to get to the essence of the thing. This woman, buried in the stage, might just be the essence of the thing.

Summer has her eyes wide open now, leaning forward. She watches the stage as though afraid to miss a secret.

Winnie has just taken a postcard from Willie. She is disgusted by the picture. *Genuine pure filth!*

But she keeps staring at the card, tilting her head to the side and frowning.

Summer wonders about the image on the prop, whether there is a real porn picture for the actors to peer at. Maybe it's a couple with a lot of hair, fucking on a shag pile carpet. Summer has a friend who makes a monthly podcast entirely about 1970s porn. The last episode was focused on outer space—silver costumes, dubious antennae, alien seduction. Summer's friend sometimes posts links to YouTube clips of the stuff. It is weird. Historical. Maybe a bit pure. Summer likes the bodily variety and the abundant bushes. She likes the straightforward performance of it, the way the sex is a show that could be cast off after the climax, unlike the first porn she saw as a teenager, made when she was a teenager, with female bodies so distorted and on task that it was impossible to imagine them doing anything other than mechanically opening their denuded vulvas or closing their epic eyelashes against a string of flying cum. Summer likes the '70s lack of silicone, the occasional awkward gestures, the faces that retain the capacity to express. She also likes all the un-tattooed flesh— its vast blank canvas—although she could never admit that to April.

April has several insects (a honey bee with a piece of comb, a dragonfly, a Christmas beetle, a trail of ants with one carrying a crumb) and three Victorian hot-air balloons and Roald Dahl's Matilda (the Quentin Blake version) inked onto her thighs. Even more significant than her leg pics are the internal organs on her torso. She has a purple heart-sized heart over her chest, its ventricles all delineated, and a pair of lovable ovaries joined by fallopian tubes between her hipbones. Lungs and a uterus, and potentially a pancreas and kidneys, are all forthcoming. April's appendix was removed in her teens so that's not pictured. And the liver, intestines, and stomach are apparently too pragmatic to warrant an external representation. Summer has recently been advocating for getting the guts out. Summer thinks guts have poetry. And April is all guts—some people would say she has balls, but those people can roundly get fucked—whereas Summer thinks of herself as lacking guts, as more of a trier. Not a try-hard, but close to that.

Summer's been trying very hard since she moved to Melbourne from Western Australia after she finished school and worked for a year to save money. She always wanted to head east to the real things. For her, the real things were bigger cities and drama school and populations that loved art unashamedly. After three auditions, she got into her second-choice acting course and then did a lot of research about cool places to live and hang out, and she found a room in a share house in a cool place to live and hang out. And then she got a job in a nearby café. The café was in a cool place to live and hang out, but it wasn't a cool café. None of the people Summer recognized from uni came into the café, although she often saw them walking past on the footpath outside. They went instead to cafés that were off the main road or cafés on the other main road (the cooler one), cafés without bains-marie or Coca-Cola fridges. It was apparent that Summer had missed the mark. She'd almost landed herself a cool job in a cool area of a cool city, but she had not.

Once she was aware of the quandary of not quite getting it right, she decided she had to try a bit harder. While she was fond of the husband-and-wife owners of the café, she gave them a hug and her notice, and found a new job as a barista at a much cooler place around the corner. She made fewer large cappuccinos at this new café, and she received smaller tips from less customers, but she was pleased. She'd nailed her move. She was living in precisely the way she'd hoped she would. Seventeen-year-old Summer would have been impressed with the twenty-year-old version of herself in Melbourne. Her seventeen-year-old self would have assumed that her twenty-year-old self was an effortless local being effortlessly cool in a cool place to live and hang out.

Since then, Summer has remained on the correct trajectory. She now has her ushering job—a perfect complement to her acting. She is twenty-two years old, about to start the final year of her drama degree. She is in love with a beautiful, gutsy tattooist. They share—with three friends—a single-fronted terrace house with some intact Victorian iron lacework and a porch, close to a train station. She can cook delicious food with kimchi and a variety of whole grains. She has friends in bands, friends who make online literary journals, friends who make podcasts about 1970s porn, for fuck's sake. Her teenage self would be bursting with pride.

But Summer is seeing a therapist for anxiety. Despite what her teenage self might think, Summer is not effortlessly cool. She is not effortlessly anything. Performing in the right way each day is exhausting her.

Some mornings it takes Summer an hour to choose an outfit and even then she leaves home feeling all wrong about some detail. She both desires and despises being appreciated for the way she looks. She can't get past that. She can't get to a zone where she is immune to the impact of other people looking.

She always thought she was feminist—if feminist means

noticing the patriarchy and resisting its assumptions—but she's begun to think she isn't a complete kind of feminist. She wears makeup and shaves her armpits and her lower legs.

She has mainly loved girls but has fretted about relationships with all sorts of people in ways that are humiliating and undignified. She is unsure if she's properly intersectional. She is left-wing but perhaps not left-wing enough. She doesn't understand the minutiae of corporate capitalism although she hates it instinctively. That said, she dabbles in fast fashion and recently bought a synthetic, bang-on-trend, cheap dress, possibly made by a child slave, which she has not been able to wear for longer than a few minutes because of the guilt.

She signs online petitions almost weekly—usually related to Aboriginal rights, sexual assault justice, or refugee policy—but she knows this is considered to be self-consoling armchair activism and perhaps worthless. She has participated in only two political rallies—the time her mum took her to the Indigenous reconciliation march when she was a preschooler and, just recently, a climate change protest with friends from uni. Her large group—actors, artists, musos—got a lot of attention from the media that day with their witty, surprising placards and harmonious chants (delivered by people with performance skills and singing voices). Summer wore a cardboard koala mask that covered her whole face and got damp when she shouted about extinctions.

She cannot discern what to care about the most. She cares too much about all the things. She votes in elections—there have been a few in her adult life—after extensive policy research and reading. But even then she has been swayed by a candidate whose look she liked, who didn't seem to be an arsehole, even if their record on live sheep exports was a bit patchy.

She is a vegetarian but she is not vegan, so there is also something incomplete there. She likes to eat eggs and cheese. At the supermarket, she scans the egg cartons with an app she's downloaded that alerts consumers to whether the chooks who laid the enclosed eggs are truly free-range or if their output has been mislabeled by an immoral farm that seeks to take advantage of the bleeding-hearted. Once, Summer scanned five different free-range cartons and each of them received a disapproving beep as a picture of a sad hen flashed onto her phone. She buys expensive milk because she vaguely understands that milk shouldn't cost next to nothing, and she hopes that her milk choice is correct. Cheese with animal rennet is avoided, although sometimes the mode of rennet is unspecified, and then she chooses the cheese that was produced closest to home, to honor the bigger picture of sustainable food miles.

She loves acting and being on stage but she often thinks it's a vacuous thing to pursue and that if she were a good person she would aspire to be in the caring professions. As part of her degree, she is allowed to choose one subject from any other faculty at the university and last semester she chose to study an eco-literature subject. Each week she read novels about surviving the apocalypse or transforming into a bug or engaging in warfare against toxic agri-business, and part of her felt fascinated and hopeful and part of her felt absurd and ashamed for reading books when the earth is dying.

And she loves her mother, certainly, but not enough. Her mum raised her alone, so she should be much more grateful, but she'd like to know about her biological father and his family, even though that is probably selfish and unnecessary in the grander scheme of things. She has imagined a time after her mother's death when she could do the discovering she wants to do without insulting or hurting her.

Some days, Summer ends up curled in a ball, bawling, with April saying the same kind things she has said to her before, the same kind things that Summer can never hear and never remember.

One night, a few months back, April said something different. Maybe you need to talk to someone, Sum.

Now she is talking to someone each fortnight (free, subsidized, a service for students). Her next appointment is tomorrow.

But who knows what is going to happen tonight? Who knows if the talking will change or stop because of something that might happen tonight? Who knows if she will have anything to say tomorrow?

On stage, Winnie is talking.

She is talking about talking.

She is talking about talking into a *wilderness, a thing I could never bear to do—for any length of time.*

She is talking about feeling grateful to Willie for being there, despite his barely animate responses.

She is talking about the potential of him.

The potential of an audience is enough, apparently, to sustain Winnie until the sun goes down.

The simple and exalting possibility that someone might notice her impeccable daily performance.

Three

vy's skirt is riding up more than she remembers it doing the last time she wore it. It's tailored, tight, the color of aubergines in a still life. Standing, it rests above the knee. Sitting, she may as well be wearing hot pants.

She lifts herself off the seat just enough to fit her hands under her thighs and tug the fabric down.

She is relieved to no longer feel the upholstery on the skin of her legs. Ever since she was a teenager in a too-short school uniform sticking to a tram seat, Ivy has sought to no longer feel the upholstery on the skin of her legs.

On stage, Winnie is considering her performance.

. . . even when you do not answer and perhaps hear nothing, something of this is being heard.

What is listening to her? Who is watching her?

Ivy watches Winnie's pale hands plucking at the grass on her hill. She pinches some tiny stumps and tickles her fingers along the grass, stops and pinches some more. She inspects the depleted patches.

Ivy received two free tickets in the post weeks ago. She doesn't need free tickets. She can afford to pay the expensive price to see the play but the theater company wants her money so she was given free tickets. The theater company wants vast sums of her money and, by ensuring that she doesn't need to spend small sums of her money, perhaps they are getting closer to receiving the vast sums. It is a silly game.

Hilary was the obvious person to bring along. They studied *Waiting for Godot* together in high school, an experience that marked the beginning of Ivy's passion for Beckett, or SB as she came to refer to him. That year, Ivy wrote out lines from the play in her spiral-bound project book (using a purple calligraphy pen a besotted boy had nicked from the local news agency). She tore out the pages (using a wooden ruler she'd owned since primary school) and stuck them inside her locker so she could get a dose of the play's potent blend of dread and confusion each time she opened the door.

Hilary has enjoyed mocking Ivy about this for more than two decades. She has mocked the fundamental fandom. She has mocked the particular fandom. She has mocked the purple calligraphy pen and the ruler.

Yes please to seeing another SB play with you, Hilary texted Ivy. It's been too long! And she added several emojis—rolling eyes, laughing tears, an old man, a pen, a pile of books, a plump red heart.

Ivy and Hilary have lately been using a lot of emojis in their messages to each other and are unsure if they are being ironic when they do so. Ivy suspects that feeling confused about whether one is being ironic is a key indicator of approaching middle age.

Ivy is in the center of the audience with Hilary on her left and a baby boomer couple on her right. The male baby boomer has the bald head and pasty skin of Willie on stage. The woman has a helmet-y brown bob.

He is asleep, and snoring. She is awake, and silent.

Another engaged woman beside an unresponsive man, Ivy thinks.

Along with Ivy, the couple will probably be guests at the drinks reception at intermission, where the VIPs will be served as much vintage Moët as they want to drink while the kids who queued at the box office at 8 a.m. to get a $17 student ticket in the back row of the theater may or may not join another queue at the lobby bar for some lukewarm white wine at $12.50 per glass.

It is only since becoming wealthy that Ivy has received so many expensive items for free, or been gifted them, as the PR people would say.

Earlier, as they waited in their seats for the play to begin, Ivy was talking to Hilary about this paradox.

I get free tickets. Free drinks. Occasional enormous floral bouquets with an invitation to another event. Last week a gallerist gave me a sculpture that I fully intended to buy. This morning

I popped into a shop to buy some perfume—I had a meeting in the building next door—and the girl threw two $50 lipsticks into the bag.

It's because you're shiny, Hilary said. Because your clothes have complex seams. And you were probably nice to the perfume girl.

Ivy was nice to the perfume girl, but she was also nice to people when she didn't have money, and no one gave her free things back then. Ivy is uncomfortable with the way wealth generates wealth, abundance delivers abundance. She is uncomfortable with that fundamental truth. She is uncomfortable with that particular truth.

I suspect you're not the only one here tonight with a new perfume, Hilary said into Ivy's ear.

A strong scent of aftershave was coming from the bodies of the young couple next to Hilary. They were leaning close together reading a single copy of the theater program. It was impossible to know whether the fragrance was primarily located on the muscular larger paler male body or the muscular smaller darker male body, or both of them. They both looked freshly scrubbed. They both looked like they'd done several laps of a heritage-listed outdoor pool late in the afternoon before dressing for the theater while sipping a well-iced Tom Collins. No trace of chlorine or sunscreen remained on their persons, just a strong peppery juniper smell. Ivy rather liked it. She was not prone to allergies.

The lights went down in the auditorium.

The scented man beside Hilary tucked his program under his

seat and apologized warmly for brushing her leg on the way back up.

Did you keep the sculpture? Hilary whispered.

Yes, said Ivy. But I transferred 17K to the gallery.

Blimey. What does it—

Bzzzzzzzz!

And the bell rang out at the beginning of the play.

The noise stopped their conversation.

Ivy jerked in her seat at the bell's sudden and extraordinary volume. Hilary patted her forearm in a reassuring rhythm as though settling a startled baby.

And they relaxed into their watching.

On stage now, Winnie, a quarter of an hour into her day— into the play—is still speaking about speaking.

I am not merely talking to myself.

Ivy should be engrossed in Winnie's every utterance but she is distracted by the snoring man to her right.

Ivy saw a production of this play in Bristol in the early noughties—the accents were all wrong—and the French version of it in the town of Roussillon near where Beckett stayed during the Second World War. Ivy thinks this Winnie on this stage now might be both the most resplendent and the most unhappy Winnie of them all. Resplendence with unhappiness is a disconcerting and captivating blend of personal qualities, but the baby boomer's snoring is advancing in decibels and Ivy cannot concentrate on Winnie's words.

The intimate rattle from this man beside her is shaking up

her brain. She is unable to focus on anything except the operation of his larynx.

She takes a deep breath and clasps her hands together on her lap.

The snoring continues.

Why is he even here? Why come to the theater at all if you're just going to use it as an opportunity for a nap?

Ivy has had enough. Her fingers let go and she elbows the sleeping man in the upper arm.

He coughs in a gurgling, ghoulish way.

She glances at him. The waxy consistency of his skin is tight and masklike, and his eyes remain closed. His snoring proceeds with vigor.

She should've gone in a bit harder. Maybe in a moment—if the rattling continues—she will try kicking his shin. She imagines his shins would already be mottled and bruised, and without much padding for armor. His shins would feel a blow to them in a way his upper arm may not. Yes, that's a plan, Ivy thinks. That is what I will do.

The man's wife does not seem aware of his snoring. Do spouses stop hearing such noises after a certain period of cohabitation, in a process of cumulative, self-preserving stupor? Is that a brilliant adaptation of our species? Ivy hasn't been married long enough, either time, to find out for herself.

The snoring man's wife is gazing at the stage with compressed lips, ignoring him.

Winnie too is gazing ahead with compressed lips. She is stoic.

She is having a happy day. She is buried in the ground but she endures. Things could be worse. Apparently.

Ivy is intrigued by this mound of dead grass that Winnie is stuck inside. It is deader than Bristol and Roussillon. It is the deadest dead grass of them all. And the light on Winnie is harsh. It is harsher than Bristol and Roussillon. It's the harshest harsh light of them all. The earth is deader and harsher now. We humans, all of us, are stuck on a dead planet with extremes that are more extreme. We humans, all of us, have to distract ourselves with denial and busy business. But it is also the Australian summer. Maybe the harshness is due to an Australian production team with a higher threshold for glare.

Ivy thinks of the man she saw last weekend tolerating his three grandchildren burying him at the beach, and how he remembered his lack of hat, his exposure to the sun and its burn, and tried to get the attention of the shoveling children, asked the shoveling children to get his hat and to put it on his head—Not that way, no, that way, so I can enjoy the damn view while you're shoveling—and then called them again when the hat blew off, the soft terry-toweling bucket hat, and the shoveling was finished and the mound around his body was patted down hard and trickled with seawater to shore it up and make it heavier and more secure before the hat was reinstated on the grandfather's head—Not that way, no, farther back, don't cover my eyes, you little brats!—and the children moved to decorating mode, running through the seaweed, searching for shells and arranging them on Grandpa's sand in rows and spirals, organized by the eldest child according to color and scale and type (did she know Andy Goldsworthy's work, or was it instinct?), and then adding seaweed, draping one of the thickest, darkest tangles of it across his shoulders and arranging a thread of emerald beads on his white hat for the final theatrical touch.

Ivy missed the beginning of the mound building around the grandfather so she didn't know for sure where his legs were inside the sand. They were not straight out in front of him, bobsled-style; that was apparent from the angle of his spine. Perhaps he was cross-legged or kneeling. He seemed to be—if Ivy were forced to commit to a single descriptor—virile. One of those old blokes who still has the firmest handshake, the most muscular body, the veritable twinkle in his wrinkly eye. A lifelong Catholic—fortunate never to have been molested—on his knees under the sand in a familiar position of prayer? Or a late-life yoga devotee—the classes are full of gorgeous women!—cross-legged in a perfected Padmasana?

When it was time for him to be released, when he'd had enough of the water views and the sun, he released himself with a ferocious roar. A slight movement was discernible in the mound before cracks appeared and then craters and collapse, and the grandfather stood up—jumped up, actually, in a mimic of the final step in a burpee—arms aloft, sand and shells sliding off his bare skin and his swimming trunks like too much seasoning on a hot chip. By the time Ivy adjusted her sunglasses to see what was happening next, Grandpa had tackled a child to the ground and had him pinned down on the bright sand with his knees, both of them whooping joyfully.

Could Winnie make her earth tremor until she roared upon release? Could she lock in her core/activate her buttocks/pull up her center or do another jargon fitness exercise to aid her escape?

It doesn't seem to be something she is attempting.

But we don't know how long she's been here. She could have tried kicking out the ground one day days ago or repeatedly for days on end, but she's declared today to be a happy day because today she is potentially being heard so today she is going to be still and speak. She is going to be still inside the ground and speak against the horror that has befallen her.

But she is worrying about her hair.

Did I brush and comb my hair?

Willie has gone away, invisible behind Winnie's hill.

Winnie is rummaging in her black bag again. Her spectacles are back inside the bag.

Her hat, with its curve of elegant plumage, is still perched on her substantial updo. The hat is a bird on a bird's nest, obviously. The black feathers on the hat remind Ivy of a boa, something a precocious toddler might fling around his shoulders after pulling it from a dress-up box.

Winnie's bag is simply that. A bag of props for play. Some props to prop her up. Emotionally. Metaphorically.

Just hours ago, Ivy was with her mothers' group in the community room they book for their monthly catch-up. All the eighteen-month-olds were pink-cheeked and irritable with the heat. They had to be peeled out of their prams on arrival, limbs tacky with sensitive-skin sunscreen. It was still morning and the smoke haze hadn't yet descended. Extreme heat and toddlers was hard. Smoke haze and extreme heat and toddlers would have been enough to cancel the catch-up. But it was the morning, so there they were, drying off under the meager air con, complaining about sweat and rashes.

Ivy kept offering Eddie his sippy cup. He'd have a few sips of water before flipping it upside down, somehow releasing the valve, and pouring the contents into a pleasing puddle near his knee. He'd swish his fingers around in the water on the lino, grin at his mother, and thrust his chin into the air to giggle at his own ingenuity. Ivy would then fill up the cup from the sink in the nearby kitchenette. Eventually she was able to distract him by pulling out a toy box.

The children gathered around the box to rummage through hats, glasses, masks, and scarves, pulling them across their bodies and waving at themselves in the large mirrored cube, covered with smudges, in one corner of the room. A hairbrush discovered inside the box caused some controversy. Eddie and his favorite friend, Anya, squabbled over it, taking turns to hold it to their heads and enact a form of wonky grooming before the other child snatched it back. Someone else's mother bent toward the two children and spoke—Gentle, gentle, sharing, that's right. Anya and Eddie kept up their squabble.

Eddie's eager possessiveness was a surprising performance

given that he was very resistant to hair brushing at home. He'd duck and weave like a mini pugilist to avoid contact with any brush being wielded by an adult hand. Ivy should probably let him do it himself and not worry about the tangled bird's nest that would result. She should give him the opportunity to self-groom, to encourage his independence, generate a sense of personal agency, and, most crucially, develop resilience.

Resilience seems to have become the key performance indicator, the K-P-bloody-I, of successful child rearing. No one talked about resilience the first time Ivy had a baby, but nowadays it was touted in every guideline from infancy. The introduction of solid food impacted on resilience, as did the use of dummies, swaddles, baby carriers, bottles. Playgroups weren't for playing; they were for enhancing the resilience needed to manage the challenges of social interactions among peers. It's never too early to learn how to bounce back from disappointment, kiddies! We mustn't let those bad feelings prevail!

Look at Winnie on stage, sitting up in her hill. Now, she is a resilient human being. Delusionally so.

But for a panicked moment, Winnie has lost track of her hairbrush.

It is in her black bag. She is upset that she returned it to her black bag. She does not remember returning it to her black bag.

But normally I do not put things back, after use, no, I leave them lying about.

She is reliant on her routine. She must remain precisely conscious of her gestures and her objects or it will not be a happy day.

Ivy thinks of Eddie squabbling over the hairbrush at play-group, his desperate clutching of it and his tormented wailing when he had to let it go. She smiles in the dark. Only a toddler or Samuel Beckett could optimize the existential loading of a hairbrush.

Oh, you, my beloved SB. Ivy has loved him for years, the mode of her devotion adjusting according to her life's circumstances and the extent of her self-consciousness.

There was a time when her share-house bedroom featured a giant poster of Beckett aged in his seventies—deep wrinkles, thick gray hair with not even a remotely receding hairline, a pair of round spectacles oddly perched just above his eyebrows. He wore a dark suit, a white shirt, and a thin black necktie. On his shoulder was a quotation from his work that the type of people who liked quotations liked best—motivational, decontextualized, typographically neat.

I can't go on, I'll go on.

Ivy bought the poster at a large sale in the student union building on campus, finding the image after flipping through hundreds of plastic folders. SB was in the same section of the sale as River Phoenix, Jimi Hendrix, Kurt Cobain. Ivy also bought a psychedelic picture of a dolphin jumping toward a rainbow as a present for a friend who was experimenting with acid. The dolphin had bulging cartoonish eyes and a glittery dorsal fin and was a more expensive poster than Beckett.

Ivy pulled down her SB picture after a further year of tertiary education bloated with critical theory, once the idea of idolizing a dead white man had become too embarrassing to have on public display.

But after uni, as a twentysomething backpacker, Ivy dragged Hilary to Montparnasse Cemetery, to pay homage at Beckett's burial place. The gravestone was fittingly gray, a single granite slab shared with his wife, Suzanne, of the brilliant surname Dechevaux-Dumesnil. Ivy was impressed with Suzanne and her work with the French Resistance. She was also impressed that after Suzanne died in July 1989, Samuel died only five months later, as though they shared one of those touching symbiotic relationships of the spectacularly old and monogamous. This was before Ivy read the biography.

Ivy took a photo of the granite grave—SB's middle name not included, Suzanne's extra row for all her letters, their matching death years, and a reflection of Ivy's sneaker on the edge of the shiny stone.

Willie, don't lie sprawling there in the hellish sun, go back into your hole.

Willie has been exposed for a while now and Winnie is again concerned for him. Her concern for him is greater than the concern she has for herself. Her concern for him seems an odd deflection of her own greater predicament. He doesn't, by contrast, seem at all bothered by the fact that she is trapped inside the earth.

Not head first, stupid, how are you going to turn? . . . That's it . . . right round . . . now . . . back in . . . Oh I know it is not easy, dear, crawling backwards.

Winnie is talking to Willie like he's a toddler whose toddling is delayed, as if his gross motor skills could do with a pediatric gymnastics instructor and a scrupulously designed obstacle course. Moving backward is an important skill, Ivy knows that. If active children can move backward—to go from a high place to a lower place—they will transition safely. Going headfirst is a bad idea. It's reckless, ill-considered, injury-generating.

Ivy's Eddie is not an advanced mover. His head size is disproportionately large compared to the rest of his body—a heavy load—meaning stability is elusive. It might still be a while before he will walk independently. When the health nurse told her this, Ivy laughed and kissed Eddie's large orb of a skull, mumbling motherly platitudes about his enormous brain.

You took that well! said the nurse, which struck Ivy as a very odd thing to say.

Eddie often drags himself across the floor, or crawls up on his forearms like a pudgy Komodo dragon. There is a child in his playgroup who stood and marched almost a year ago. There's a bum shuffler who cannot seem to tolerate any weight bearing on her legs. There are neat crawlers who move like wind up baby dolls, nodding their heads rhythmically as they progress across the floor. There are a couple of others who cruise—clutching insistently onto supportive furniture or walls—rather than letting go and standing up. Alone. On their own two feet. Ivy watches the children, their variable ways of being, and thinks that they hardly look to be all of the same species.

Ivy wasn't meant to be allocated a mothers' group after Eddie's birth because she wasn't a first-time mother. The maternal health nurse knew her history and assumed she wouldn't want to attend meetings to learn about things she'd already experienced.

But I'd like to make friends, Ivy told the nurse. Locally.

The nurse was surprised, but amenable. Well, of course, dear!

And so Ivy was granted access.

The first meeting took place in a fluoro-lit room upstairs at the library. All the babies were six weeks old then and the mothers arranged them in a circle on a large mat on the floor. Eddie fell asleep. Several others wailed and clenched their fists. The maternal health nurse stood on a green plastic chair and took an aerial photo of the infant mandala.

You'll never forget this first meeting!

The nurse reminded them that they were a parents' group, not just a mothers' group, and that she should probably be known as a parental health nurse, but tradition persists. She was visibly enthused by her own modernity.

Was she an idiot? Every other adult in the room was a post-natal female.

She was right, of course. It is traditional for women to be pregnant, not men. For women to give birth, not men. For women to breastfeed, not men. Please fuck off with your parenting. Can't we be called mothers anymore? Not even when we're perched here with vaginas just healing after weeks of sitting on spiky stitches and oversized clot-catching sanitary napkins? With our breasts dripping blood from grazes and milk from straining ducts?

Can't we be what we are, just for a time, before we bring the men back into it? Before we accept this parenting label, as if we're all living in a state of disembodied, post feminist, gender-blind teamwork?

The women smiled agreeably at the nurse. They were women and they wanted to be agreeable. It was only later, when the nurse left the room, that they made acerbic comments.

Look at me parenting, laughed one mother, shoving her enormous breast into her daughter's open mouth.

My boyfriend's going to come to the next meeting and tell us his birth story, said another. His poor body is still recovering.

My husband, Matt, walked to the shops with Eddie in a carrier, and three strangers congratulated him for being a great dad. Eddie was asleep, Ivy added. The shops are around the corner from our house.

Ivy made friends that day. Locally.

At the third group meeting, the nurse called on Ivy to provide some advice about swaddling. What do you think, dear? You're an experienced parent.

Ivy's new friends looked at her, confused.

So she told her story.

My first son, Rupert, died of SIDS when he was almost four months old. He was asleep in his bassinet at our home in Paris, and he didn't wake up. That was sixteen years ago. I was in my twenties. Yes, it was as bad as you imagine.

The women who were holding their own babies pulled them closer to their chests. The women who were not holding their babies leaned forward and lifted them off the floor rug, tucking their two bodies, big and small, tightly together. Some of the women had a rush of instant tears they wiped quickly from their eyes. They asked all the questions.

No, the bedding wasn't wrong. He wasn't suffocated under the bedding.

Yes, he was wrapped and on his back.

No, there were no soft toys in his cot.

Yes, he was a smallish baby.

No, he wasn't a premature baby.

Yes, it was normal for him to have a long sleep at that time of the night. But this sleep was too long.

I smoked cigarettes at home—only on the balcony, but still—and I was a bit drunk when I found him. That doesn't have anything to do with his death. I was just starting to see that my first marriage was a mistake. Rupe and I were going to leave. That was my plan. My drinking was strategic then. I'd feed Rupe and then throw a shot of whiskey down my throat and tell myself it was out of my system by the next feed. I needed those small pockets of blur.

A photographer took photos of Rupe's body after he was taken to the hospital. Those photos were delivered one afternoon by a hasty courier who flung the large envelope through my front door. I didn't know what was inside that envelope and when I opened it, the grief was like a wave of nausea that surged through every part of me. I liquefied. There was nothing of me that wasn't pouring. I disappeared. I was drunk for a few years. And drugged. Whatever I could get my hands on. I spent a lot of money on mostly very effective chemicals. Eventually my best friend, Hilary, dragged me back to Australia and forced me to live with her until I resurfaced.

But Ivy didn't say those last things to her new friends. Not then.

Instead, she offered them reassuring statistics on the odds of having a baby die suddenly while asleep. She squeezed her own healthy new son, performatively, lavishly, until he let out a high squeak in declaration of his undoubted aliveness. She didn't want to make the women feel any more frightened than they already were, as new mothers.

Fear is the first lesson. There is a fear that settles into you as soon as pregnancy starts. It might be gentle or it might be raging but Ivy knew it was in them all.

Ivy smooths down her skirt across her lap. There are tears covering her face and she smooths her cheeks as well, pressing her palms down on her skin as though to blot away the moisture.

She doesn't want Hilary to see she has been crying. She doesn't want to upset her.

Ivy thinks of a scene in a novel she recently read about a man so disconnected from his own self that he cannot recognize the saline wetness covering his face. He says something vaguely hilarious, vaguely tragic about the unexpected lachrymal event he is experiencing before realizing the odd fluid is an expression of an internal sorrow, that he is in fact—what is the term?— weeping. Ivy never fails to recognize the fluid on her face but, occasionally, still too often, she is surprised to find it there, and she thinks the difference between not knowing what it is and not knowing when it got there is only the smallest progression of conscience.

She wishes she were more evolved, more aware and in control of the tenuous boundary between what is concealed and what is not. She thinks this leakage is a developmental flaw, that if she were properly adult and competent, she would not cry in public. She would wait and be appropriately private rather than have her feelings spill out all over her.

Ivy concentrates on the woman on the stage.

Fear no more the heat o' the sun, the woman says. *Did you hear that?*

Yes, I heard it, Ivy thinks. It's Shakespeare. *Cymbeline.*

That line's also quoted in *Mrs. Dalloway*, and Ivy is fairly sure it was in another novel she read not long ago. And here it is again.

Why does she remember things like that? How does that help her with anything, in the slightest?

Can't contain tears. Can contain detailed information about books.

Now Willie is yelling back at Winnie. *Fear no more!*

He is yelling back half the line, half of what she said to him, and for that, Winnie is very grateful. She appreciates his paltry efforts to engage with her words and provide a kind of response.

Why? Why is she grateful for that?

How does it help her to be grateful for that, in the slightest?

Four

Margot's cough is under control for now but the air conditioning remains a problem. The thermostat is set very low, and Margot's body cannot settle in the cold. Her legs are crossed at the knee and then twisted again at the ankle. The black handbag on her lap is a practical cat, providing a welcome patch of warmth on her thighs. Margot is cuddling the bag.

The silly pair on stage is squabbling over a line from Shakespeare. She wants his attention, and he is giving it to her, in his partial and irritated way.

Willie's response is not what Winnie needs and it is not enough. She is trying to talk herself into gratitude when it is obvious to Margot that Winnie feels only disappointment.

Winnie is trying to be glass half full. She is thinking herself away from her immediate, deeply felt emotions, to focus on the bloody tepid half puddle of water in the bottom of the chipped dirty glass, instead of the large empty space above it. But she is unconvinced.

Doubt.

   Here.

      Abouts.

Winnie places her hand on her chest, over her ball gown bodice. She adjusts her fingers, locates the heart, and presses down.

Her white hand is bright in the harsh light.

There are doubts somewhere in the vicinity of her heart. She can feel them.

She is holding them there.

Heart doubts. Waverings. Confusions.

Margot is hearing this declaration of doubt.

Or is it a confession, to express doubt? An accusation?

It depends on who is listening.

Doubt has not played a large part in my own life of the heart, Margot thinks. At least, not until the goings-on of the last couple of years.

Once Margot adjusted to the affronting nature of her pregnancy with Adam, that momentary lapse in control, she sorted out her contraception. Done. She never doubted her decision to have only one child. Adam was enough. Her heart expanded just enough in the way she hoped it might when she was worried about becoming a mother. I hope my heart will expand just enough and the love will make it right. Well it did. There was no doubt.

And she never doubted her choice of husband. John was enough. She wasn't one of those foolish people with lofty ideals about their long-term romantic relationship, believing that a single other human could be the most socially exciting, the most spiritually sustaining, the most intellectually stimulating, the most domestically capable, the most physically inspiring, emotionally revealing person they know. John wasn't everything to her. But he was enough.

They were both brainy, the professor and the surgeon, like the beginning of a bad gag. People might assume that the bond between brainy couples is primarily intellectual, that their bodies are only storage spaces for their minds. That's not the case for John and Margot, not at all. She keeps her deepest thinking to herself, or for her work. She talks to him, of course she does, but he has never been her essential intellectual sounding board or, how ridiculous even to consider it, her muse.

But physically they are merged. It is physically, in the realm of the limbs and the flesh and the ooze and the shudder, that there is no barrier between them. He is her lover, absolutely.

How I love his body, she thinks, if not all his bodily functions.

In the early days, Margot realized that their sex life was a refuge and a revelation. Getting into bed together was exciting and comforting, both. What a gift that was.

But they don't read the same books, or always want to pass time in the same way. And gradually, as the years went on, she realized different things touched their souls, if one is allowed to speak of souls anymore.

In such a long union, you work it out. You take what you have and don't dwell on the missing of what you do not, if you intend to endure it.

Margot thinks now of the Saturday many years ago when she used John's car because hers was at the mechanic. There was a Romanticist visiting from Canada who was staying with his relatives in a bayside suburb. The relatives thought it would be fun for some of his local colleagues to come over for a classic Australian barbecue. Margot accepted the invitation, and packed a potato salad and a bottle of riesling. John wasn't interested in joining her, preferring to remain at home for the afternoon watching the football telecast.

When Margot walked out to the front of their house, got into John's car, and turned on the ignition, the car stereo blasted. It was playing rock music—a man singing, steady drums, guitars. The volume was up very high.

She didn't know the song or the singer. Her instinct was to turn off the stereo but she stopped herself from doing so. Instead, she sat there in the idling car as the music continued.

She listened to the man's voice.

She felt the bass thump thump thumping in her chest.

She imagined John getting into the car, choosing the music, pressing the up arrow on the volume controls, pulling away from the curb, and steering down the dip in their street, singing along, knowing all the words, maybe dancing in his seat and throwing his head around as he accelerated into full gear. And it was a small revelation.

She hadn't even known he kept CDs in his car. If she'd been pressed to think about it—and she never had, why would she?—she would have said John listened to the radio (the cricket, the football, the news) when he was driving alone. But he listened to music. And there was something about the emotional thrust of the song and the volume of the stereo that made her understand plainly that when her husband listened to music, it made his heart soar. It filled him up.

She looked around for a CD case and soon found a pile of them in the glove box on the front passenger side where she sat when they were going out together. She rarely opened the glove box, only to get a tissue, and she had never searched its contents. Why would she? She pulled out the colorful cases and sorted through them on the passenger seat next to the bowl of potato salad she'd placed there for the drive.

One of the CD cases was empty. Bruce Springsteen, *Darkness on the Edge of Town*. So that was what was playing.

John liked to drive and listen to Bruce Springsteen very loudly on his car stereo. Okay. Well. Now she knew.

It changed nothing between them. Margot did not mention it. She did not start buying John CDs as gifts, watching him unwrap them and smile at her thoughtfulness. She left him alone with it, his secret blasting soundtrack. He could have it to himself. If he'd wanted Margot to share in his soul's love, he would not have kept it private. She knew it would have been a mistake for her to intrude, perhaps even disrespectful.

She turned off the CD and drove quietly down the street.

She remembers feeling grateful for the substantial and silent drive out to the Romanticist's relatives' house, for the time it gave her to recalibrate her understanding of her husband. She was swift in locating a bottle opener for her riesling upon arrival. She also remembers that.

Oh I know it does not follow when two are gathered together . . . that because one sees the other the other sees the one, life has taught me that.

The woman on stage is concerned about being seen. She is calling to her man off stage—hidden behind her mound—and asking him to see her.

He does not see her. He does not reply to her.

Her parched mound is feeling especially tight today, as if her body has gained some weight inside the hot earth. She strokes the dry, bright hill stretching out from her torso, rubbing her hand back and forth across the slope as though caressing her own hugely distended belly.

The woman is trapped inside a landscape that is garishly explicitly brutally harsh and she is afraid she cannot be seen by her man. What a distortion of reason!

It seems to Margot that people are rarely afraid of the right things.

So many women of her vintage are concerned about becoming invisible, for example. If Margot reads another opinion column lamenting the invisibility of older women, she might just scream. If it is true, it can be a relief. What a whole lot of extra energy we all have when we are not expending our social resources managing unwanted attention, when we no longer—thank god!—have to take care all day not to offend some idiotic male with his idiotic male commentary. Why complain about all that falling away?

That said, I haven't lost it completely, Margot thinks. If I have to wait a bit longer to be served in a shop, fine, I'll speak up, but that doesn't mean I'm invisible. I'm still trim. I know how to dress. I've still got energy to flirt and the wit to follow it up. It's the attitude that matters. As my dearly departed mother liked to say, you get the face you deserve. So I've got frown lines from thinking and laugh lines from laughing, and that's fine. The people I knew who were dreary at twenty are just drearier at seventy. The dynamic young people are now dynamic old people. Why isn't that more widely understood?

Margot thinks of Maggie, her dear friend with the almost matching name. They've known each other for fifty years, and Maggie has become increasingly vain as the decades have passed. She makes nasty comments about other women almost reflexively, pointing out their flaws. She spends huge amounts of time recovering from surgeries, getting her nails done, getting her hair done, getting matter injected into her flesh, even getting eyelashes implanted in recent years.

She was always nervous about losing her looks and, according to her logic, losing her husband as a consequence. And she was—Margot has no doubt about it—afraid of the wrong thing. Her husband lost interest in her—that's been apparent since the '90s—but that was because she became mean and boring, not because she became old and dumpy. Her focus was entirely skewed.

Margot has also been afraid of the wrong things.

With John, she was afraid of two things—him being unfaithful and him deteriorating physically—and neither of those fears came to pass. Perhaps because she was sexually possessive of John, Margot had elaborate fantasies for many years about being cheated on and the precise ways she would discover his infidelity—handwritten notes revealing kinky sexual quirks, the proverbial lipstick on the collar, a frank conversation with a mutual acquaintance (I think you need to know what's been going on)—and then the revenge moments she could enact—the destruction of favored clothes, art objects, or books, the placement of a sliver of sardine inside his suit pocket, the rubbing of his toothbrush around a toilet rim in the hope he might get gastro—and the delicious, enlivening moral high ground she could occupy as she explained to him what a terrible cliché he was, what an unimaginative middle-aged doctor, what a weak fool, but how, even though she was betrayed and heartbroken, she might be able to forgive him eventually, depending on the extent of the illicit relationship, the person involved, and how many others were aware of his betrayal. She would want to know every detail of what had happened. She would insist on knowing every detail.

But none of that occurred. Those fantasies did not manifest.

Instead, Margot found herself cheating—kissing a man in her car one night after a party like a pair of teenagers with nowhere private to make out, then finding a scarf he left in the car, inhaling its scent, and scouring it for her own hairs before shoving it into a post-pack and sending it back to him. The kissing happened after hours of conversation where she marveled at the easy humor and candor of what they were saying, and had absurd romantic thoughts about having finally met her match, aged in her forties, in this gregarious and generous man. And then the repeat performance, a few weeks later, without the forgotten scarf—they were careful there—but with some clothes removed that time, only above the waist, but still. And more conversations full of mutual desire and confession and confusion and electricity. That was what happened instead.

And the terror of being the cheater was made much worse because it was mentally unrehearsed. Margot had spent all her imaginative energy being afraid of the wrong thing and had no idea what to do with the horror of that version of infidelity—her own betrayal, her own flipping stomach, her own blame, her own tremendous yearning for the other man that rose up in an explicit sensory memory when she was preparing a snack for Adam or sitting beside John watching television.

It didn't go far. The other man was indiscreet and too loose when drunk. One night that might have ended in another tryst, they were having dinner with a group of colleagues and he reached over to her plate and picked up a piece of bread as if he were entitled to it. She looked around and was certain that others had noticed the gesture. And, later, as people started to leave, he grabbed her jacket and began to put it on, playfully. He couldn't conceal their intimacy. And that was the end of it.

It was a glitch in her marriage, of course. Margot needed to carefully perform for a few months to disguise what was going on in her mind and her body, until it eventually dissipated. Desire, like a drug, loses its potency, and she chose not to seek bigger hits to sustain it. But even now, almost thirty years later, she can think of the other man sliding his arm into her jacket and feel a horrified buzz.

Margot shifts in her seat and clears her throat. The tickle has gone but she fancies another Fisherman's Friend. The packet crunches inside her black handbag as her fingers find the seal.

The white-haired woman sitting in front snaps her head back toward the sound, glares at Margot, and lets out a well-practiced, disapproving sigh.

Yes, I'm having another one, Margot thinks. Aren't I just dreadful?

Margot drops the lozenge into her mouth. It is quite excessively flavored. An intense menthol cool.

The young man seated beside her adjusts his position. His forearm remains on the armrest between them even as he shifts. It's as though the young man has glued his skin to the velvet upholstery, so unrelenting is the placement of his arm.

On stage, the woman is excited about an insect she's spotted. *Looks like life of some kind! An emmet!*

She is peering at it with a magnifying glass like a preschooler with a new bug-catching set.

An emmet. What an odd word. A synonym for ant?

It's just an ant that has crawled across her mound. A lone ant.

If Winnie squashed that ant, would it smell like eucalyptus? Would it have an aroma like Margot's lolly?

The stink probably depends on the species.

Margot thinks of the time she discovered the odor of ants, how confusing and obvious it was that they should smell that way.

She was a little girl, maybe seven or eight. They had driven the cream FJ out to a spot far along the Yarra River, close to where a fire is burning tonight. She thinks of the cramped spiky undergrowth beneath a canopy of eucalypts. She thinks of the paths through the bush that they were allowed to run along, the louder the better to scare the snakes. She thinks of the gravel car park and the old towel her father spread across the front windscreen of the FJ to block out the sun, and the nearby clearing, surrounded by gum trees, where the grown-ups set up plates of food on timber picnic tables with attached bench seats. Many of the plates of food had wire mesh domes over them to keep the flies away. Perhaps there was a round chocolate cake that wasn't veiled, decorated with a frothy twig of red bottlebrush, picked for the purpose upon arrival. Perhaps it was someone's birthday.

Margot stood on the roots of a tall eucalypt, hugging the tree's trunk to maintain her balance. It was hot and her favorite cousins were late to arrive. Margot picked at the bark on the tree, pressing her fingerprints into a pliable dollop of toffee-colored sap, and she felt a tickle going up her legs, under her skirt, toward her undies. She put her hands down to scratch and felt the movement of ants. She lifted her hands up in horror. There was a bit of ant under her fingernail. There were ants in her pants!

She screamed and started jumping up and down, up and down on the dry and dusty ground. Her sandals were brown with firm straps across her toes and ankles. Crumbs of earth flew up around her sandals each time she landed. Her already-dirty dress was pale blue with a short full skirt that ballooned as she jumped up and down.

Margot's mother walked her away from the gum tree, into the clearing. She poured some water down Margot's legs and told her to take off her pants and shake them out. Margot stood near the timber picnic tables and the domed food and the exposed chocolate cake, shaking her undies like a rag in the breeze, with her bottom bare and bitten under her skirt.

Once she'd put her pants back on, been sat on a bench and both laughed at and consoled, Margot looked at her fingers. She picked out the piece of ant that still remained under her nail. The aroma of eucalyptus was strong.

Later in the day, once the ants-in-the-pants story had been told to every new arrival at the picnic ground and Margot had perfected her crazed reenactment performance, she found some more ants and squashed a couple and sniffed them. Yes, that astringent aroma was her clearest memory of the day she got ants in her pants when she was a little girl.

Margot thinks deliberately now. Was she the little girl who got ants in her pants? Was it actually her?

Or was it her sister who'd attracted the critters?

Or was it Adam in his footy shorts when they went to

Wandiligong that Australia Day long weekend when she was on sabbatical?

Was Margot the person who poured the water down the small sticky legs? Was it she who stopped the child jumping and squealing near the tree?

Margot doubts most of the memory now. Apart from the smell of the ants. That part is so definitive she can taste it.

Margot sucks hard on the lozenge in her mouth.

The woman on stage is watching the imagined ant through her magnifying glass and notices it is carrying a white ball. An egg!

Well then, Margot thinks, this parched land isn't as barren as one assumes. Perhaps there is hope here that the woman will be released, that the man will embrace her, that the brutal heat will dissolve and a gentle trickle of water will darken the thirsty ground.

As soon as an egg appears in a text, you know you're being asked to pay attention to questions of fertility and burgeoning life, motherly nature, Mother Nature, fecund or precarious.

Margot likes to point this out to her students—note the egg! The observation always gets a bit of a laugh. She likes to remind them that a single egg on a dining table has all the loaded potential of Chekhov's gun. There's nothing arbitrary about its presence, not usually.

I'm certainly remembering a lot this evening, Margot thinks, pleased. Nothing wrong with my brain. How gratifying it is to wallow in one's thoughts. It's worth keeping up the subscription for this alone, this quiet pleasure of being compelled to sit in a theater for a couple of hours a few times each year, uninterrupted and contained.

But I lost a train of thought somewhere, Margot thinks. I lost it to the emmet and the egg.

Ah yes. Being afraid of the wrong things and, with John, there are two ways my fears have proven to be misdirected. I was afraid of the possibility of his infidelity and the possibility of his physical deterioration. I didn't think of my own infidelity, which didn't amount to much in the end, or the possibility of his deterioration taking a different form, which has amounted to a great deal.

Short-term memory loss.

Long-term memory loss.

Confusion regarding everyday objects and actions.

Mood swings.

Physical aggression.

The physical aggression is meant to happen only very late in the game and, even then, it is statistically uncommon. But John is still mostly lucid, still able to talk about his prognosis and sometimes even laugh at himself.

Most days, there are only lost seconds or minutes. The doctors say there might be years yet before he starts to lose hours. The doctors say the violence is an anomaly. The doctors say Margot needs to monitor it and manage it. The doctors say avoidance and escape are her best strategies.

Early in her marriage, Margot liked to test the extent of her love for John. She would lie in bed with him, usually curled up together (he was a man who enjoyed nocturnal entanglements, even in the heat), and ask herself the most difficult questions she could think to ask.

Would I still love you if you were paralyzed from the waist down? Yes.

Would I still love you if you were paralyzed from the neck down? Yes.

Would I still love you if you were fitted with a colostomy bag? Yes.

Would I still love you if you had erectile dysfunction? Yes, we could get a little pump or something.

Would I still love you if you had severe facial disfigurements? Yes.

Would I still love you if you gained fifteen kilos? Yes.

Fifty kilos? Well, I'd suggest a fitness regime, but yes.

What an inane little idiot I was, Margot thinks. Obsessed with the physical. And what a tiny repertoire of fears.

How about this for a real question, Professor—

Would I still love you if you punched me? Yes. As a matter of fact, I would.

Her young self would be horrified by the question, and even more horrified by the answer.

It's not that simple, Margot tells her young self. The doctors say he is not responsible. And I'm tough, you know that. And quick.

Margot's young self isn't buying it. I've got some more questions for you, Margot's young self is saying.

Why have you told no one—not a single person—if it is simply a medical issue?

What if his diagnosis is an excuse for the enactment of some previously latent desire? Have you considered that maybe he's always wanted to hit you?

And what if you lose your cool? What if you defend yourself, lose your cool, and kill him?

Margot shifts in her seat. Coughs a little. She does not want to keep thinking about John. She must stop thinking about John.

She notices the armrest between herself and the young man is finally free. The young man has his arms crossed now, palms wedged into pits like he's posing for a team photo.

Margot places her bare, cold arm on the armrest. She mirrors the position with her other arm on the free armrest on the other side. She concentrates on feeling queenly.

On stage, the woman pulls her revolver once more from inside her black bag. *You again!* Oh, why couldn't she have pulled out her lipstick? Margot doesn't want to think about a revolver.

The woman is holding the gun in the palm of her hand, feeling the weight of it in her fingers and through her wrist. The gun is such a dark solid thing in the light white of her hand.

Margot held a gun once. It was heavier than she expected it to be. It was probably about six, seven years ago? Yes. They had been out for dinner in the city to meet Adam's new girlfriend, Grace, who worked in the state government's communications department. She often worked late, especially if a government minister had said something careless in public. That day, Margot remembers, the health minister was outed as a committed smoker during a tour of a children's hospital refurbishment. Could be worse, he told a group of journalists and TV cameras. At least I'm not an ice addict! He was a complete twit, a real bumbling boob of a man, and now Margot could not think of his name.

Grace was determined to keep the dinner plans, so they met at 9 p.m. at a Portuguese restaurant near her office. She only had to cross one wide road to get there. The three of them were already seated when she arrived. Adam and Margot were making derogatory comments about the kitsch religious iconography covering the walls. John was bending awkwardly in his chair to get the attention of the waiter.

It was late winter and when Grace came inside cold air rushed into the restaurant, blowing over a long-stemmed iris in a too-short vase perched on the corner of the bar. Margot remembers being struck by Grace's beautiful jade woolen coat and the pair of expensive French spectacles she was wearing. Adam was her optometrist. That was how they'd met.

I imagine it could feel quite intimate, having someone examine your eyes, Margot said to Grace after a couple of wines. If the person who's doing the examining is as handsome as my son, of course!

Oh, Mum, please, protested Adam.

But Grace took the bait, agreed, and giggled. He put some drops in my eyes on our second date. He just stopped in the middle of the street when I said my eyes were feeling dry and pulled a little bottle out of his bag. Then he tilted my chin up with his fingers and told me to watch the clouds as he released two perfectly targeted drops into each eye. My eyelashes fluttered at him, I'm sure of it, explained Grace. I almost literally swooned!

Margot clapped her hands together. Wonderful!

Margot remembers the tipsy debrief with John in the taxi on the way home from dinner. Grace was ideal. Easy conversation. She was smart, but not too smart. She was attractive, but not too attractive. Nice, open, warm. And she was elegant, too, which was lucky for a person with Grace as a name. What an imposition it would be to have an adjectival name that didn't fit one's character.

The cat was on the porch when they got out of the taxi. That was the first hint that something was awry. Her eyes flashed in the dark, confused. The hall light was off when they opened the front door. The hall light was almost never off. They walked into the dark house and switched on the lights.

Margot's underwear was all over their bedroom floor. Jewelry from the underwear drawer, cash from the cutlery drawer, a large jar of spare change from the mantelpiece in the lounge, a new iPad still in its box—all gone.

A window into the kitchen had been forced open, and was still open. The stone kitchen bench was cold and wet with rain as Margot leaned over it to close the window. John was annoyed she touched the window, hectoring her about evidence and fingerprints. (Have you considered that maybe he's always wanted to hit you?)

John called the police, who told him they would come to the

house the following morning. Margot put her strewn underwear in the washing machine, fed the cat, and went to bed.

The next morning, John had scheduled surgeries and left early, and Margot was working from home on her Eliot book. She had a tight deadline, so tight she probably shouldn't have gone out for dinner the night before.

A pair of police officers arrived almost two hours after the scheduled time. They were both very young, very tall, and very polite. The male officer had wide womanly hips. Margot watched the way his blue trousers pulled across his rear end as she followed him down the hallway toward the crime scene.

The officers explained to Margot about a spate of recent robberies in the area, and the opportunistic nature of thieves who see an empty house—they would have rung the doorbell, found the window, been in and out in a few minutes. They explained the ice problem motivating the burglaries, and the current lull in supply after a customs seizure.

The woman was a forensics officer. Margot showed her the kitchen window and the relevant drawers and left her to take some prints. The male officer said he'd have a look around the house and confirmed that it was okay for Margot to return to her work.

After a few minutes, the male officer stood in the doorway of Margot's study. What was taken from in here? he asked.

Nothing, she said. As far as I'm aware. Blessedly, not her laptop (probably too old) nor any of her first editions (probably too specialized) had been stolen.

76 CLAIRE THOMAS

Is this how it normally looks then? He frowned at the piles of books, papers, and folders all over the study floor.

The piles were not neat. Many of them were collapsed into long diagonals that seemed to violate the laws of physics in that they were still any sort of pile at all. There were two floral upholstered armchairs pushed up against a large, full bookcase. Their seat tops provided an upper layer of horizontal surface for several stacks of papers. Piles of art books, their spines all facing different directions, filled the lower layer on the floor underneath the seats.

Yes, said Margot. It's a total shit heap! She liked to swear in front of blue-collar men. It helped to develop a rapport.

The police officer laughed. Well, whatever works for you.

Can I hold your gun?

I beg your pardon, madam? He stood up straighter then and lost his smile.

I've never held a gun. Would you mind?

And to Margot's astonishment, he obliged.

She put down her pen as he made his way toward her, stepping through the mess, finding some gaps for his feet on the floorboards. And so she sat at her desk in her daggy gray cardigan, holding the police officer's handgun aloft above her Eliot manuscript. She'd been editing chapter seven on *Daniel Deronda*. Margot didn't grip the handle of the gun or put her finger anywhere near the trigger. Instead, she rested it flat on her palm—the short barrel pointing out alongside her thumb—just like the woman on stage.

The next time Margot saw Grace, she told her, almost con-spiratorially, about the police officer's gun, making sure to men-tion that Grace was the only person who knew about Margot's audacious request and the officer's compliance. That shared se-cret got Margot off to a great start with the person who would become her daughter-in-law. Grace told Margot she had chutz-pah, which struck Margot as an unusual way for a young Chi-nese Australian to describe an older Anglo woman. But chutzpah was definitely the word Grace used. Even all these years later, Margot remembers that.

It seems that the woman on stage is now properly contem-plating her fate. She's tired of her thwarted attempts to commu-nicate with her husband and is talking about gravity, the fact of her entrapment, the inescapable material conditions of her existence. Good-o, thinks Margot.

. . . if I were not held in this way, I would simply float up into the blue . . . some day the earth will yield and let me go, the pull is so great, yes, crack all round me and let me out.

Margot recently had the extraordinary feeling of floating out of her body. She was on the selection panel for an entry-level academic position in her department and the panel had to watch the five shortlisted candidates present their future research plans. Around the time a young scholar was attempting to explain the productive difference between representational literary charac-ters and typological literary characters, Margot astral-projected toward the white paneled ceiling and hovered over the scene like a harrier hawk. For a moment, she felt a blessed buoyancy, a complete untethering, as though all the talk from below could just float around her in a cooling irrelevant vapor.

But then she fell back into herself.

She fell back into the room and the responsibility and the requirement to suspend her own growing disbelief about the value of all this research, all these delusional graspings toward intellectual exceptionality.

That brief flight was a lovely pause, Margot thinks. But I don't want the earth to let me go. I want to be grounded. I rather like the force of everything I am weighted with.

During hectic periods at the university, Margot imagines slipping into a different life, a lighter one with fewer people, fewer schedules and expectations, in which she would live somewhere remote but faintly cosmopolitan, a tree-change town where you could buy a decent jar of olive tapenade and find a well-scheduled yoga class. She'd own a sensitively renovated period cottage with great proportions. She'd spend hours reclining in a cozy bay window reading novels, occasionally looking up to admire a gorgeous magnolia tree in her effortlessly thriving large garden. She would be unencumbered. John, the old John, always featured in this alternative life, interrupting her reading to show her a curious meteorological map on his iPad or to hand her a gin and tonic made with liquor from the local boutique distillery fifteen minutes along the main road.

She feels a shiver of embarrassment to realize now that Adam and his family haven't made it into her fantasy, her rather conventional image of retirement.

Well, it doesn't really matter. I have no intention of retiring or disappearing into the ether anytime soon, despite what that upstart of a dean might be encouraging. I don't care about an academic succession plan, about making space for the next generation of scholars. Those pressures are just fresh ways to disproportionately burden a senior female with mentoring responsibilities. I can think of several old men—gray fixtures in the faculty—who haven't developed a new research proposal or lecture in years, and I bet they're not losing sleep over the brilliant young minds who can't secure an academic appointment. I will continue with all of it for as long as I please.

Margot has paused once or twice during her career to reflect on her frenetic disposition that manifests as compulsive busyness. Perhaps it is a decoy to avoid the truth of herself?

She considered seeing a psychoanalyst but she couldn't commit that many hours of her time to such a dredging. Such a drudge. And she was put off by the thought of several of her younger male colleagues, laden with Lacan worship, unable to have an un-theorized encounter without allusions to a sublimated signification chain.

So she'd seen a clinical psychologist. A man with a couple of decent degrees and a kind face. What a waste of time that was! The psychologist told her that a person is defined, ideally, not by what they have done but by who they are. Internal fortitude is the source of healthy self-determination, not the external affirmation of others, ideally. The psychologist told Margot she should strive to have a sense of herself that is about core values, an understanding that is not contingent on achievements or activities or even—and this is where he really lost her—her relationship to others.

Perhaps that would be possible if one did not achieve, if one were inactive or a hermit. So she imagined being someone without a professorial chair. Someone who had not written several books. Someone who had not won many prestigious awards and grants for her work. Someone who did not have friends and colleagues whose good opinion she craved. Someone who did not get invited to speak at international conferences. Someone who did not have institutional and cultural power. And those erasures were only momentarily tolerable before she felt panicked and bereft.

She grappled, as instructed—yes, that's what she did, bloody well grappled—with the psychologist's notion and tried to accept it. But it was horseshit. How is anyone able to differentiate between the being and the doing?

If I do nothing, aren't I also nothing but a passive repository for my intellect and emotions and bodily functions? Doesn't the doing activate the being, and give it form?

Ha! said the clinical psychologist. You are not the first high-achieving person to suggest that to me.

Smug bastard. So she made it simpler for him. The components of my life cannot be deducted like fructose or gluten in some sort of elimination diet. I don't believe in an ideal core of healthy selfhood that will only thrive once we get rid of all the superfluous things that might be damaging me. Get it? He got it.

That was several years ago, when Margot's life was so fundamentally unproblematic that she was able to define her own hyper-functionality as a problem. If Margot had seen the clinical psychologist more recently, would she have told him about her career confusion? Her husband's illness? About her son's contempt? Would she have made a point of wearing a sleeveless top to the consultation in the hope that he might be the only person ever to ask her about those awful bruises on her arms? And might she have just told him the lot, and cried, and listened to the sound of her own voice saying out loud all the shameful thoughts that were whipping uselessly around her brain?

Does she need to hear it all said out loud?

On stage, the woman has picked up a parasol. She is fiddling with its mechanics and is unsure whether now is the right time to open it. She is unsure whether she should further endure the heat until she becomes even more desperate for the shelter of the parasol. She is unsure whether prolonging the opening of her parasol might help her to get through the day. Perhaps it is just too soon.

Oh, put the damn thing up and protect yourself, Margot thinks. What on earth are you waiting for?

Five

Summer watches the slight shade falling on Winnie as a parasol rises over her body against the glare of the blazing sun. Like stepping under a full tree on a stinking-hot day, Summer can almost feel the glorious relief of that shadow.

But the parasol is not a tree, and Winnie is not a mobile human being, and she is not relieved. *The heat is much greater.*

Winnie is dissatisfied with the parasol's protection and she cannot adjust it so that it will provide sufficient relief. She swaps the parasol to her other hand, and gives it a try from a different angle. *Holding up wearies the arm.*

All she has is her arms, poor lady. No wonder she doesn't want them to feel tired.

It's odd, Summer thinks, how quickly your arms start to strain when you hold them up. She went to a trial Kundalini class one night and the part she remembered most—the only part she told April about when she got home—was when they had to hold their arms out to the side at shoulder height. She experienced a surprising low-level pain that necessitated some committed focus to maintain the pose. She can't remember what her legs were doing but they weren't a problem. Only the sideways arms.

Gravity's a bitch, April laughed. Then she walked to the doorway between their bedroom and the hall and stood inside the frame. Did you do this when you were a kid? I just remembered it.

April had her arms by her sides and then she raised them a bit, pushing the backs of her hands hard against the inside of the door jamb. She held her hands there, exaggerating the pressure she was placing on the jamb before she stepped forward, away from the door, and her arms floated up up up as she stood with a dreamy smile.

Summer did the trick in a different doorway opposite April. This does feel nice, she said, her wings rising toward the ceiling.

Winnie cannot seem to give up on the parasol, despite the weariness in her arms. She cannot put it down. Perhaps it's a mechanical issue. She had some problems putting it up in the first place, and now she cannot put it down.

Perhaps there is no defect with the buttons or the pop or the slide of the parasol. Perhaps she just doesn't want to relinquish her glimmer of hope that there might have been some respite from the harsh white light that surrounds her.

So still she holds the parasol, her face folding against the glare.

I cannot move, she says to Willie as though this is news.

Winnie wants Willie to tell her what to do. She is used to being compliant with his wishes, and maybe a feeling of relief might come, not from finding some shade but from her own submission to a man. Love and obey and all that jazz.

She calls out to Willie again. He is nowhere to be seen and he does not answer her pleas. So she holds the parasol.

And suddenly it is ablaze.

There are tall flames coming out the top of the open parasol.

Summer is impressed with this each time she sees it, but to-night, tonight it seems wrong that they went through with it at all. Maybe they should have decided to skip the flaming parasol, just for tonight. Winnie could have pretended that her prop was on fire.

Summer thinks she can sense some discomfort in the audi-torium.

She looks around.

There is a subtle shifting of bodies, a little current of tension. I can't be the only one in here who is worried about the fires out there. Surely there are many of us. Or maybe nobody is that stressed about them. Maybe they'd all forgotten about the fires until the flames appeared on stage, and now the remembering will last for just a moment. It is impossible to know.

When Summer is sitting in the audience like this, she often wishes she could get into the heads of the people around her. She wonders if they are taking any notice of the play, or if they are sitting here having irrelevant tangential thoughts, or if they are busting to go to the loo, hanging on until intermission.

Winnie throws the parasol behind her mound, out of the audience's view, and twists her torso so she can watch the flames quickly flicker away in the dirt. *Ah earth you old extinguisher.*

But the earth is not often an extinguisher, Summer thinks, crossing her arms over her chest. Only the wettest or barest earth would extinguish a flame. Much of the time, the earth embraces a fire. It allows its crispy cover of plant life, dead and alive, to fuel a fire's beginning and enlarge it. The dumbest arsonist with a cigarette butt has worked that out.

April told Summer about a kid she went to school with who always had a thing for fire. He volunteered for the CFA, lit regular almost-too-big bonfires in his dad's backyard, the whole bit.

But everyone knows he's one to watch now, April shrugged. The local cops make sure someone takes him to the movies or somewhere on high-risk days. There's always one like him. They're a cliché for a reason.

I understand the appeal, Summer said. I could stare at fire for hours.

April laughed at her. Oh, babe. Not the same thing. At all. You wouldn't harm a fly, much less set fire to a forest.

Thinking about that conversation now, Summer feels the blood rush to her cheeks. I would harm a fly. I'd whack it with a tea towel until its dark hard body fell to the floor. Then I'd probably stomp on it. So there.

April is much less efficient with fly killing. She runs around with a can of spray, squirting fumes everywhere until the fly is in a spinning frenzy on an inaccessible bit of the floor. She takes forever. Summer used to let April do all that but lately she's stepped in with her superior skills. She opens a nearby window or door and guides the fly outside—usher-style—or otherwise it's the whack-and-stomp approach. Summer quite enjoys the whack-and-stomp. It's the closest thing to a surge of mastery over nature she has ever felt, and it's enough for her. She isn't about to start shooting ducks for a hobby.

Last month, Summer and April went to the Botanic Gardens to participate in an art piece about human beings needing to get over themselves and to *rethink their spurious attempts to dominate nature*. The project's intentions were clearly explained on a sign set up outside the information center at the gardens.

It was about *the afterlife of our bodies*. It was about *how we humans are only as relevant as our ecologies, not its rulers*.

Summer wasn't sure if that final sentence made any sense, but she was open to the experience.

Summer and April arrived at the gardens early, and waited in the gift shop full of Christmas decorations featuring native fauna and flora. After a few minutes of wandering through the shop, making fun of the festive Australiana, they approached the registration table in the information center foyer. There was a girl sitting there who knew April from work. There was very often a girl who knew April from work.

The girl swung her leg onto the tabletop, over the EFTPOS

machine, the paper printout of bookings, and the pile of mobile sound devices.

April, she drawled. Look at how well this has healed. She rolled up her baggy linen trousers to reveal a large tattoo on her calf muscle. It was a bird and a branch—a beautiful kookaburra and a sprig of pink flowering gum.

Oh yeah, it looks great, said April, before introducing Summer to her client.

It was bleeding for a while, the girl said, after nodding in Summer's direction, her leg still propped on the table. The scabs were so bad I wasn't sure if it was ever going to look any good. But now it does. Now I love it.

It looks like a Christmas decoration from that shop, Summer thought.

It's gorgeous, Summer said instead, holding on to April's arm.

They registered for the art experience and were each given an iPhone with clunky headphones attached. They were told to follow the park ranger to the specified area in the gardens and not press play until they were lying down under the trees.

They walked behind the park ranger in a chatty group of about twenty eager art-goers. The ranger offered long plastic mats to anyone who was anxious about getting dirty (no one was anxious about getting dirty) and then they all lay down under the trees. Everyone chose a good spot for their bodies in the copse, like the courteous way that strangers (unless they're creeps or weirdos) arrange themselves in an elevator. No one was awkwardly too close, and an aerial view of the scene would have been nicely balanced.

Summer and April lay side by side, put on their headphones, and did a countdown to ensure that their audio was in synch.

Three, two, one, PLAY.

You are the center of a scorched island, a British voice announced.

Scorched islands seem to be a theme of Summer's summer. She remembers that precise line among the many images in the long calm monologue about decomposition. The idea was to consider your own body as a corpse, lying on this patch of land, rotting into this earth, with the process explicitly described by the voice.

Blood is pooling in the parts of you touching the ground, along your back, your buttocks, arms, and legs, and this is how that pooling blood would look on your skin—dark, drastic bruising—and this is what might remain contained, and this is what might seep out into the earth.

Summer found that idea particularly disturbing—the body as a receptacle for fluids that settle inside or leak away, according to pressure, gravity, outlets—but now that she thinks about it, isn't that what we are when we're alive anyway? We are always only just managing to keep all the liquids inside us.

As well as blood and other fluids, gases are produced and dispersed as the corpse loses solidity, all of it interacting with the ground and the atmosphere. Many insects were discussed, the trees overhead, the birds, the other strange and estranged beasts that might assist or benefit from the decomposing human island. There was a grim mention of a *multigenerational mass society of maggots*. And, finally, after an imagined epic time scale, *your bones become stone*, the voice declared. And it was over.

Summer stretched her body and stood up. She pulled out a stick from her hair and threw it onto the ground.

A man nearby did a goofy dance for his friend as if to perform his un-deadness.

They're not eucalypts, April said, standing. They're big ol' oaks. And she rolled her eyes at the expansive trees surrounding them. The voice in the recording mentioned eucalypts several times but we're under oak trees.

When they were returning their headphones, April asked the park ranger about the trees.

The artists are British, he smiled. They updated the piece for Australia with the gums, but they might not have known it'd be taking place in an oak circle in a colonial garden.

There are eucalypts on the other side of the gardens, aren't there? April asked.

There are, said the ranger. But insurance. Risk assessment.

They looked at him.

Oaks are less likely to lose a limb, he said. And kill someone.

Summer and April left the Botanic Gardens and walked out onto the street, past the massive stone Shrine of Remembrance, a monument to lives lost in war. During her first term at drama school, soon after her arrival in Melbourne, Summer had sat inside the shrine, flirting with another acting student, drinking ciders he'd been carrying around in his backpack for hours. It was almost midnight and he was a local boy who said he wanted to show her some unexpected views of his city. The view from the shrine that night had definitely been a good one with the spread of light from the buildings making Melbourne look like a proper metropolis in the clear sky at the end of the boulevard. They got in trouble with the aggro security guard patrolling the shrine and were told to move on and show some respect, as if they'd been having sex or vandalizing the walls. No offense, Sum, the local boy said, but I've been here a few times and never been told off. The local boy was blond and white, and Summer held his hand as they laughed and jogged away from the security guard and away from the monument to lives lost in war. They passed piles of crocheted red poppies propped up alongside plaques dedicated to desolated battalions, twee crafted reminders of blood spilled on battlefields. Summer saw those red poppies in her peripheral vision under the orange glow from the streetlights and wondered if they'd last longer there on the ground than her memory of that Melbourne view or her flirtation with the actor.

Thinking now, it all feels so tangled together—the local boy, the stone shrine, the security guard, the crafty poppies, the art piece, the girl with April's tattoo, the lost soldiers, the trees, buried bodies, death, decay, the whole damn lot. And now Summer is watching a woman on stage pretending to be stuck in the earth and the woman is crying out to her mute companion, concerned that he is not replying, concerned that he might be unconscious, which seems an overreaction to being ignored but understandable given the poor woman must be absolutely losing her mind. Summer is feeling worried, so worried, but she cannot work out if she's worried about Winnie, or herself, or the blazing world outside, and where the blood is pooling or spilling at this moment, inside a certain body or beyond it.

Breathe, Summer. Remember to breathe.

With the sun blazing so much fiercer down . . . Shall I myself not melt perhaps in the end, or burn.

On stage, Winnie seems to be talking about climate change, but she can't be talking about climate change, Summer thinks, because the play was written sixty years ago and I am just being paranoid. I am just hearing her words that way.

Did I ever know a temperate time?

What the hell is going on? At intermission, I will call April. Somehow I will get downstairs to my locker and call April. What if she's driven to the mountain to help Joe and Maureen? To take Woolf safely away to the lowlands? Would she risk the drive? She always says that there are more roads in and out, on and off the mountain than most people know. But April knows the roads. What if she decides to do something heroic? What about a wind change? A lightning strike? Anything could be happening up there.

It's okay. I will go to my locker at intermission and find my phone and get in touch with her. If a supervisor notices I'm gone and I get in trouble, too bad. I'm not sure this job is good for me

anyway. I have too much time in my head. Maybe I should quit
and go back to the café, where my hands were busy and all I had
to do was smile and talk shit to people so they felt special about
their coffee order or their outfit or their new hairstyle or their
holiday. Maybe that was better than having all this time sitting
still inside a theater with my stupid, anxious head. Uni will be
starting again soon and I won't have so many shifts. That might
help. Or not, because then I'll have less money and every single
thing I do or don't do will be about whether I have the money to
do or not do it—getting a tram or riding my bike, buying food,
paying a bill, seeing anything, going anywhere, every tiny thing
every tiny day—and that feels like a huge clamp screwing into me
or a clichéd gray cloud hanging over me, threatening to pour
down. And being an usher is good for my cultural education, of
course. If the teachers at uni knew how ignorant I was about theater, they never would have let me into drama school or passed me
through to third year. I didn't even know what this play was
about until last week. I thought Beckett was always crusty old
men complaining about being alive. During first year, a couple of
boys performed a dialogue scene from *Waiting for Godot* and that
was the extent of my knowledge. On opening night, when I realized this play was about a woman buried in a mound of earth, I
was embarrassed and amazed all at once. So I'm learning here. I
am. I really am. But I have so, so much more to learn.

On stage, Winnie pulls a music box out of her black bag. She
winds it up with a small key, opens its glittery lid, and grins. It is
a child's box with a pale pink ballerina stuck in a permanent

pirouette. The harsh stage light bounces off a round mirror in the open lid and across Winnie's eyes and cheek as she looks inside. Music plays as the ballerina turns around and around. Summer doesn't know the tune.

Summer thinks of the music box her grandma, her mum's mum, gave her when she was a kid. The pale pink ballerina in her box wore a red tartan kilt instead of a stiff white tutu and, instead of the melancholy waltz coming from Winnie's box, Summer's box played a cheery Scottish folk song.

Summer's mum's mum was always very pleased about her heritage—a Scottish father on one side and sixth-generation settler Australian on the other. She liked to refer to the Scot in herself as though it defined her character. I love a drink, she'd say, but I don't much like paying for one!

During the last few years of her life, the old lady became enthused about researching the family tree. Summer remembers when her grandma discovered that she was descended from a pair of First Fleeters, that they were all descended from a pair of First Fleeters. She sat Summer and her mum on one side of her Formica kitchen table and clapped her hands together, raring to the tell the story.

Nathaniel and Olivia were both small-time thieves in England. He might have been framed, they think, not actually a criminal, but Olivia was the real deal. Armed robbery, the works! They both went to trial and were both spared death and sentenced to transportation to the colonies. They both arrived in Australia on the First Fleet, different ships, and were both then chosen to be part of a new settlement on Norfolk Island. They didn't know each other until they moved to the island but they knew each other fairly well soon after. They had the first of their eleven babies—eleven babies!—within the year, before a minister from the mainland was able to travel over and neaten up the domestic arrangements—marry the cohabiting couples, christen the infants, consecrate the already dead and buried. There were six more children in quick succession for Nathaniel and Olivia, including a set of twins. Now—let me stop here and ask you a question. What do you know about Norfolk Island? What do you think of immediately when you hear Norfolk Island?

Colleen McCullough, Summer's mum answered.

No, no.

Pine trees? Summer suggested. Like the ones at Cottesloe?

Pine trees, yes! yelped the old lady. Exactly. One day, Nathaniel was trying to clear some pine trees around the settlement with fire—a controlled burn, I suppose we'd call it now, but very small-scale—and one of the biggest pines didn't behave as expected and fell to the ground in the wrong direction. Its huge trunk landed directly on the family house—a crushing, flaming load. The twins were killed, a few days before their second birthday. Another child suffered several broken bones and Olivia walked with a limp for the rest of her life. She managed to have a heap more children, so she can't have been too wounded, but still. Those little twins, both of them killed by a damn pine tree, can you imagine! What a story, eh? That's our family. Six generations back on my mother's side. Half the current population is probably descended from their offspring, but still. It's a quintessential Aussie story.

Summer's mum was embarrassed by her own mother's fascination with the family tree. I don't see why it's interesting, what any of it's got to do with us all living now, she said.

And, as if to compete for dramatic impact, she told Summer another family story at a different time. The two of them were watching TV, a nature doco about Scottish birds of prey, with heavily accented voiceovers and vistas of expansive wings.

Here's something about the Scottish heritage on my mum's side of the family, Summer's mother began, out of the blue. My grandfather, Mum's father, was born in East Fife, the last of twelve children. The day he got on the boat to migrate to the other end of the globe was the day he found out that his eldest sister was really his mother. No one had mentioned it to him before. They were all just getting on with their lives—poverty, World War I, et cetera. It was only when he was saying goodbye to his family at the dock that he was handed his birth certificate and learned the truth. His sister's name was listed under Mother, there was a blank space under Father, and stamped in red ink at the bottom of the page was a single word—BASTARD. In red ink. Can you imagine?

Summer laughed, aghast, and fixed on the TV as a peregrine falcon ate the face of a pigeon.

Summer rarely opened her tartan ballerina box after hearing that story. She didn't feel connected to anything Scottish or balletic but she could definitely relate to BASTARD. She felt like a fragile twig hanging off the family tree without an identified father of her own. There wasn't a red BASTARD on her birth certificate but there was a blank space instead of the name of a man. Summer knew nothing about him and she gave up asking a couple of years ago, once her mum had provided a single detail after a long bout of nagging.

No, I was not raped, she told Summer. You are not the product of a rape.

Isn't that reassuring? Isn't that a special piece of information to hold on to?

I definitely have a lot to learn, Summer thinks. Starting with who the hell I am.

Summer's face is burning hot, despite the air con. She adjusts her body in her chair and folds her arms across her shirt.

Breathe, Summer. Breathe. You're okay.

The fires will be okay. April will be okay. I will call her at intermission. Or I will check the emergency updates on that app. Her parents will be okay. They know what they're doing.

But Summer imagines April driving up to save Woolf from the fire, her beloved mongrel baby. April chose her as a tiny puppy from a rescue center in the outer suburbs. It was her twelfth birthday and she was increasingly moody and antagonistic toward her parents. The puppy gave April an excuse to go for long solo walks through the forest, away from Joe and Maureen. April named her Woolf because she'd just finished reading *A Room of One's Own*, an experience that probably hadn't helped with her growing moodiness and antagonism. Woolf was an unlikely name for a scrawny puppy, until she grew up and developed a formidable bark. Woof woof, little Woolf! After a decade of devotion, April moved to the city and decided to leave Woolf with her parents. It's for the best, April often said, trying to convince herself. She's a mountain dog, and she wouldn't be happy down here with me and my tattoo life.

But occasionally, when Summer and April are hanging in their city neighborhood, they will pass yet another pampered pooch wearing expensive knitwear, going for a walk with an owner wielding a plastic ball-throwing tool and tugging a pink plaited lead, and April will get teary. Oh, I miss my baby, she will say, after giving the pedigree pup a vigorous pat. My baby could show these posh dogs a thing or two.

April loves Woolf abundantly, maternally, despite or maybe even more so since they no longer live together. Thinking about it now is scaring Summer.

She remembers reading in the news about two girls who were killed trying to save their two horses in a bushfire several years ago. They were always described together—the four of them— as though the death of a girl was equal to the death of a horse. Four lives lost. Or were they described in that way because the girls and the horses had become almost indistinguishable? Had their mutual devotion merged them into a hybrid species? An equine-girl. A fem-horse. The girls' parents were almost fatally injured trying to save their daughters, after their daughters had reached their horses, in a desperate chain reaction. Did the parents later wish that they'd never brought up their kids in a place where the love for an animal can be as dangerous to the human individual as the love for a child? The same inextricability between self and other. The same blind impulse to rescue.

What if Woolf is freaking out and barking and running around like a nutty mutt in the smoky heat? Surely, she'd be restrained while Joe and Maureen did their thing, chasing the spot fires. Would she be locked inside, or tied up outside? Would she know to drink water and lie on the concrete in the carport to keep cool? Are dogs able to sense when a fire is on the way? Can they hear something or smell something that humans cannot detect?

At a farmers' market once, Summer bought a carton of eggs from a man who'd lost all his chickens in a bushfire.

They knew something was wrong before I did, he told her. They all started running around in circles before the first embers even reached our property. I lost all my fencing and shedding that day, the works. But I rebuilt my business. And now my chooks live in the lap of bloody luxury 'cos the sight of their burned friends covering my paddocks, well, that's something I'll never forget.

Just this morning, Summer read an article about tens of thousands of flying foxes dropping dead out of trees in heat waves around Australia. There was a picture of their leathery bodies in a large pile, and a close-up shot of a bat's face, a stock photograph from before the heat stress, replete with pointy teeth, staring eyeballs, and a furry, furrowed brow. And just before the flying foxes, there were the mass fish deaths in the northern river system. Bloated cods, hordes of them, lining the exposed riverbanks or bobbing along in dirty, shallow flows. That was about reduced water levels, algal blooms, something something.

Summer heard different people in the media, when trying to make sense of the mass deaths, explain both cases in the same way.

Those flying foxes are the canary in the coal mine.

Those fish are the canary in the coal mine.

Even the adorable polar bears in the Arctic have been described as the canary in the coal mine. What the fuck? That symbolism messes with Summer's mind.

What does it mean that certain dead animals are considered a warning sign of actual danger? Does it mean that those certain dead animals, the canaries, are dispensable, but whatever might die after them is not? Does it mean that real danger is only the demise of the creatures we care about—ourselves, animals we're personally devoted to, super cute animals, captive animals that humans depend on for business?

I suppose human beings pick and choose the other human beings they care about, Summer thinks, from all the billions of human beings on earth. It follows that we might do the same with all living creatures.

But what about the species that are recently extinct? Isn't the fact of their demise a fairly solid sign that we're all already in trouble? Do we still need to fixate on localized catastrophes and call them the damn canary? The canary has long fucking flown, or dropped off its perch, or whatever the hell it does. The canary can retire. We don't need any further warnings. The end is already here. The end is not still pending. The end is not some manageable little problem that a human being can master and deflect like a pesky fly. Fuck it.

Summer is sweating. Her neck is wet beneath her heavy ponytail. Her face prickles. She holds on to the top of her trousers with her wet palms, her fingers spreading out across her lap. She can sense the moisture on her thighs through the fabric.

There is pressure in her ears. It is a pressure that feels as though her heart is beating just above her jawline on both sides of her face, as though her heart has spread into her whole head and is now trying to beat right out of her through her ears. It is hot and full inside her ears.

She releases her jaw and opens her mouth a bit. She remembers that. And it does help. Something eases inside her skull. Something definitely eases.

And she remembers her breathing. She remembers to slow her breath.

She counts in for four, holds her breath for three, counts out for eight.

Her diaphragm shudders and resists the new pace. She keeps trying.

She counts in for four, holds her breath for three, counts out for eight. Counts in for four, holds her breath for three, counts out for eight.

Counts in for four, holds her breath for three, counts out for eight.

Counts in for four, holds her breath for three, counts out for eight.

And now she is almost breathing normally.

Her hands are no longer so clammy. She tucks her elbows in close to her sides, careful not to touch the armrests, and presses her drying palms against her rib cage. She feels the deep steady breathing in her diaphragm.

She is breathing normally.

Okay. Okay. I did okay. I'm okay.

I'm sitting in the auditorium, watching the play. Okay. My feet are on the floor inside my black Docs, inside my white socks. My feet are pressed to the floor. I am still. I am grounded.

Watch. The. Play. Just watch the woman on stage.

Winnie is worried about her fingernails. *What claws!*

She finds a nail file in her black bag and attempts to neaten them up. She is sawing away at her fingers, back and forth, back and forth, determined to inflict some change.

Willie is still hidden behind the mound but every so often Winnie leans back to take a look at him. He is picking his nose and eating it. Winnie is unimpressed and implores him to spit it out. The audience is also unimpressed. There is a low groan of disgust from the crowd, and a few sniggers.

They've been so quiet up until now, Summer thinks. Snot consumption seems to be a tipping point.

At primary school, there was a girl in Summer's class, Lottie Morgans, who used to sit on the mat while the teacher was teaching and dig away at her nostrils and feast on her excavations like it was a perfectly nice thing to do. Did Lottie ever find out that everyone referred to her as Snotty Lottie? No matter what

Lottie Morgans ends up doing with her life, she will always be Snotty Lottie in the memories of the people who knew her as a child. It's the same with the boy who vomited all over his desk on the first day of year two. Summer can't even remember his name. They were at school together for years but the only thing about him that sticks in her mind is his shocked face after he threw up on that hot February morning—his pallor, his wet eyes, the bit of sick remaining on his lip. And that girl in high school, Alex Something, with the period puddle on the back of her dress, and how she refused to tie her jumper around her waist in the way the other girls did when the same leak had happened to them. No, Alex Something was defiant about her puddle for the entire afternoon. It's perfectly natural, she said to anyone who stared. I'll rinse it out when I get home. She was probably fourteen at the most, Summer thinks. How did she get so uninhibited at such a young age?

Summer shifts in her chair. She doesn't want to be thinking about this stuff. Her ears are filling again. Her palms are feeling damp.

Inside her dry mound of earth, Winnie is inspecting her fingernails. She is pleased with them and declares them to be a bit more human.

Bit more human?

What? To file your fingernails into a neat shape makes you a bit more human? Why is that, do you think? Animals have claws, whereas human beings have manicures? Stupid fucking humans.

And before she has decided to move or not to move, Summer is pushing the heavy black door at the back of the auditorium until the seal around its frame lets out a small pop and it is open and she wobbles out into the foyer and walks into the empty carpeted space and looks up and sees herself in a wall of mirrors and she is just an usher wearing a uniform and she is there in the mirror and she is okay.

She stands alone on the carpet and looks at the person in the mirror and she is okay.

Six

vy's face is dry of tears.

The snoring from the baby boomer beside her has gone down a notch and she is calmly concentrated on the play.

Winnie was just scolding Willie for picking his nose, but she's stopped, thank god. Ivy has a real aversion to snot. It's her least favorite bodily product. She's grateful that Eddie isn't one of those toddlers with a permanent gelatinous tube between his nostril and top lip. He's been a bit of an explosive pooer and projectile spewer, but none of that bothers her. If anything, those gross abundances have been a source of comedy. It has surprised Ivy, this time around, how funny it is to have a child, to be so close to such a small embodiment of human absurdity.

In photos that Matt sends to Ivy when she's working, Eddie often looks like an adult impersonator. Reaching for a ukulele or a book with a determined frown on his face. Wearing a button-down shirt and sitting up at the kitchen table. In other photos, when Eddie is captured being who he really is—a mostly helpless human child—Ivy is reminded of other species.

He's clinging to you like a baby bonobo!

He's devouring that food like a piglet!

She is aware what a curious paradox that is, as though humanity alone has an inherent dignity.

Ivy is someone who pulls out her phone when she's inside a toilet cubicle just so she can experience the fillip of seeing that fat little face on the screen. Her second child. Adult impersonator, baby animal, comedy embodied.

She is tempted to take a peek at her phone now. She could reach down to her bag and pull it out, touch the screen, and her son would appear.

She does not do this. She will wait until intermission to have a look at him again.

She thinks about what he would be up to right now, asleep, his cheek planted on the cot mattress in a growing circle of drool, his round nappy bottom in the air, the breeze from the pedestal fan wafting over him in a comforting white noise rhythm. The crown of his head smelling like ripe strawberries, delicious. His hands—so soft they almost feel damp—in loose fists over his small sharp fingernails.

On stage, Winnie is filing her fingernails with a sense of absolute creativity, as though only she is aware of the particular shape being produced by her work. She is leaning forward into the task, peering at her fingers to assess whether the shape has almost been achieved. She registers her approval, and sighs.

Ivy has never used nail clippers on Eddie. She couldn't bring herself to put even the smallest blade on his body. When he was a new baby, she nibbled his nails herself. More recently, she's used an emery board for the job. Eddie is giggly and cooperative, especially if he's allowed to tap Ivy's legs with the long gritty thing afterward.

Winnie starts on her second set of fingernails now and is more automatic in her gestures with this hand. Her mind is released from her current task and wanders off into memory.

She is recalling the time, long ago, when a couple strolled through the wilderness and encountered her, buried in the earth, and Willie, crouched behind her mound. The couple—a man and a woman—squabbled over the point of Winnie, *stuck up to her diddies in the bleeding ground.*

What's the idea of you? What are you meant to mean?

What hideous questions to contemplate.

Winnie dismissed them as rhetorical and did not answer.

What's the idea of you? Ivy replays the replayed question. *What are you meant to mean?*

No one could properly respond to that riddle when stuck and exposed under a searing sun. Ivy thinks she might have a chance of producing an answer if she were given a quiet room to reside in for a week, or a vast landscape made of gentler material, paths to move through, and plenty of shade—those environments might be conducive to existential coherence—but the harshness of this wilderness with its ceaseless glare prevents any lucid explanation.

The answer in these circumstances can only be—to endure.

The point of Winnie's presence is to endure her presence.

The point of her here is to endure.

The point of her here is to perform her attempt at endurance.

Yes, that's it. Nothing more than that is a possibility, under the circumstances.

Winnie is recalling that the strolling couple asked further questions, beyond the existential one Ivy is fixed on.

The woman asked, *Why doesn't he dig her out?*

The man asked, *What good is she to him like that?*

And among the various interrogations, it is the practical question that is most bothersome to Winnie. *Why doesn't he dig her out?*

Why hasn't her companion attempted a rescue?

Is it a lack of desire or a lack of capacity or a lack of the right tool to help with the job? If there happened to be a shovel, with a retractable handle, snug inside Winnie's black bag, would she have thrown it over to Willie by now? Could she finally capture his attention, not with her attempts to engage him in conversation, but by giving him a practical, physical task to perform? That can be an effective method for activating the ambivalent male.

Have a go at getting me out, Willie! she might have shouted. Here's a tool from my bag!

Looking at Winnie sealed in the earth, Ivy thinks of an entrée she ordered years ago at a Michelin three-star restaurant in

Paris, back when going to such a restaurant was still a shock to her, when the distance between herself and her surroundings felt anthropological, when the only way to make sense of the strangeness was to pretend she didn't feel any strangeness and believe that she might one day relax inside such luxury.

Ivy chose to order the items from the menu she understood. I better have the *betterave*, she thought. At least I know what that is. She wasn't expecting a mini Mont Blanc. The entrée arrived on a large white plate—a small white mountain of sparkling salt. The salt glinted when the waiter placed it down on the table, the candlelight catching on the bigger crystals. The waiter picked up a piece of cutlery Ivy had never seen—similar to a fish knife or a butter knife, but bigger and without a sharp edge. The waiter used the odd piece of cutlery with an elegant momentum, tapping on the salty slope and looking up to smile at the diners. After much tapping, the small salt mountain crumbled away toward the perimeter of the large white plate to reveal a steaming, glossy, whole beetroot. The waiter explained to Ivy how the vegetable had been cooked inside the salt mountain and how its flavors—and there are many flavors, you will be surprised, *mademoiselle*—would now reveal themselves to her. Ivy ate the whole beetroot in a few mouthfuls and felt inadequate about tasting nothing but the earthy, bloodred thing itself, and the salt. She could certainly taste the salt.

The plated mountain was the same shape as Winnie's desiccated mound, with the same gentle gradient. If Willie took to Winnie's mound with an appropriate shovel and gave it a few good whacks, it might crumble away and reveal the whole of her. Would Winnie be all pinkly cooked inside her mountain? Would the full spectrum of her flavors only be revealed when her entire body was exposed?

Enough, Ivy thinks. I know the play. I know what it is doing and where it is going.

Winnie's mound will not budge even if the right implement is wielded at the right angle with the right force for the right duration. She will not be rescued or exposed. She's stuck in the earth and the sooner we all realize that, the better. Right.

She is also stuck in time.

She must endure the torture of experiencing each second of each day, with only scant and blessed glimmers when her actions become successful distractions, when her memories are absorbing, when her tight, interminable grip on reality is relieved.

The day is long, and she feels each tick.

Winnie is considering packing away her objects in readiness for night. She doesn't have a timekeeping device so she can only guess when it is appropriate to start tidying for tomorrow. Everything must get returned to the waiting black bag on her mound, so it will be there, in place, to be pulled out and considered again throughout the next long day.

It's like packing up after a toddler.

Play. Tidy. Repeat.

Play. Tidy. Repeat. Repeat. Repeat.

Winnie picks up the revolver that has been waiting on the slope beside her. Is it time to put the revolver away?

It makes sense that she'd start with the gun, Ivy thinks. It's probably got its own internal pocket in that voluminous black bag. It might not be the only object in Winnie's possession that is a potential killing machine, but it is the most obvious one, and so it is the object that most needs monitoring in careful storage.

Ivy remembers her next-door neighbor who taught her how to drive when she was seventeen. He was a father of four, Ivy was his fifth student, and his spiel was tightly honed. He described his station wagon in just that way—as a potential killing machine—on the day he took Ivy out for her first lesson.

Look at this vehicle, he said, leaning on the long beige bonnet. You've seen a production line, all those parts coming together to make a car?

Ivy nodded.

Well this here is the finished product, a vehicle for getting us places, sure, for moving us from A to B. But it's also a potential killing machine. And the onus is on every person who ever gets behind the wheel of a car to never, ever forget that. Got it?

Ivy nodded, trying not to smirk at the man in his striped polyester tennis shirt and his flip-down sunglasses, earnestly performing his adult wisdom. He was so intense about it, and she just wanted to get in the car, rest her hands on the steering wheel in a casual way, and learn how to execute a three-point turn.

Ivy thought of her neighbor again, years later, when she was in London and saw a Cornelia Parker sculpture in a free exhibition at the Tate. The sculpture was a pair of guns taken off their production line, placed side by side on a white plinth. The objects had the thick recognizable shape of a gun without any of the mechanical detail that would make them an operational weapon. Instead of machines for killing, the guns were presented as vulnerable fetuses, curled toward each other like twins in utero, prematurely removed from reaching their violent potential. When Ivy was admiring those embryonic weapons in an art gallery on the other side of the earth, her neighbor's beige station wagon drove through her mind and tooted its horn. She was a few years older, and a few years more compassionate by then, and it occurred to her that there was probably a tragic explanation for his assertions about the violent potential of a motor vehicle. Maybe he had lost someone he loved in an accident. Maybe he had killed someone himself with the vehicle he loved, the vehicle that gave him freedom until the moment its potential as a killing machine was realized. The poor bloke. She cringed at the memory of her failure to see through his bravado.

That sculpture of the not-real-not-quite-manufactured firearms is as close to a gun as Ivy has ever been—that is, not very close at all. But she would like to shoot a gun. She would like to feel the backward thrust of her body after it fires. She thinks a shooting range would be fun. One with targets that look like targets, though, rather than targets that look like people. She couldn't shoot a gun at a discernible human silhouette, not even in a controlled or imaginary way. Unless she pictured a row of racist, right-wing bigots. Maybe then she could muster up the hate needed to blast the human shapes away. But a target—a giant red bullseye—would make for an enjoyable game. She'd be good at it. She would hit that red circle every single time.

She imagines walking into a shooting range—a shooting parlor? Is that what they're called, or is that a sideshow alley game?—and being handed a firearm by a gruff ex-cop working there in retirement. There would be a lot of instructions and a lot of forms to complete. The gun would be so cold and compact that it might be difficult to imagine it as a potential killing machine, but she'd get a lecture about the danger of the thing before she'd even be allowed to hold it.

On stage, Winnie sets aside her weapon. It is not quite time to tuck it out of view. It is almost time, but not quite.

Winnie senses that the bell will soon blast to announce the end of the day, just as the bell blasted to announce its beginning. In Winnie's world, the beginning and the end are echoes. Without the relief of sleep, it takes so much longer to reach the end.

Hilary—mother of three, pragmatist, woman consistently occupied with her own complex career—used to complain to Ivy—a bereaved former mother, pragmatist, woman consistently occupied with her own complex career—about the distortions of time that occur with child rearing, and the glacial progression of the clock toward the close of the day. She told Ivy about everything she'd facilitated for her children—crafts, ball games, costumes, music, snacks, a lot of snacks.

I'm being mother of the year, Hilary said. I'm filling the

afternoon with all these exemplary activities, and then I'll look at my watch and twelve minutes have passed. That's it. My entire repertoire is exhausted and we've moved twelve fucking minutes.

After a forty-degree day when the power failed and Hilary was at home with the twins and the baby, she told Ivy that since she'd had children, it felt as though she'd lost years but gained minutes. That idea seemed resonant but Ivy lacked enough personal experience to know for sure.

Ivy was never offended by her friend complaining to her, a woman whose child had died as a baby. Ivy didn't expect Hilary to be permanently grateful for her own children. That was as unsustainable as Ivy being permanently resentful of everyone else's offspring. And they'd together experienced so many of the tenuous variables of something as apparently basic as breeding.

As teenagers, their periods synched for a whole year, and they thought that was incontrovertible evidence of the superiority of their bond among all the girls they knew. Before Hilary lost her virginity to her nice boyfriend of several months, she called Ivy on the landline for a final word of approval. Ivy's first time was more spontaneous but Hilary still knew about the event within the hour. Later, Ivy helped Hilary after she'd taken the morning-after pill and was crying in bed, violently nauseated, for two full days. Hilary helped Ivy after she had an abortion when things went wrong with a boy she didn't even like much. Later still, Hilary endured incorrect diagnoses for polycystic ovaries and an incompetent uterus—how they had milked the morbid hilarity of the incompetent organ—before she was declared to be nonspecifically challenged in terms of fertility. Ivy got pregnant within a fortnight of her decision to conceive with her first husband. When Hilary thought she was finally pregnant with her husband, there wasn't an embryo there at all, just the indicative hormones of pregnancy, taunting her.

Hilary miscarried another of her earlier pregnancies when she was in Paris, attempting to extract Ivy from her grief there. She was only ten weeks along and ill with morning sickness during the long flight from Melbourne. She hoped the sickness was a good sign, but she miscarried a week after her arrival. Hilary didn't tell Ivy about it, not for years. Not until Ivy resurfaced, not until Hilary had given birth to twins after five rounds of IVF treatment.

When she finally told Ivy about the Paris miscarriage, Hilary said that she hadn't wanted to burden her when she was already suffering so much, when Ivy was grieving the loss of—what was Hilary's phrase?—a baby who had lived outside of her. Yes, that was it. A baby who had lived outside of her. For a time.

Ivy cried when she found out, at the thought of Hilary, pregnant and then not-pregnant, in pain and desolate, unable to speak of her joy or her loss due to Ivy's own state of unreachable and buffering intoxication. Such was their friendship.

Thinking about this now, Ivy reaches over to Hilary's leg in the dark and gives it a pat. I bloody love you, she thinks.

Hilary glances at Ivy with a fast smile before turning her head back to the stage. She is watching the play.

Hilary's profile is lit up in the glare of Winnie's sun. She has pulled her hair back tonight in twists. At intermission, Ivy must remember to tell her that the twists look nice.

On stage, Winnie waits for her day to end, and Willie emerges once more. He struggles to crawl across the earth.

The hands and knees, love, try the hands and knees.

Willie is an old man, his motivation as deteriorated as his joints, and Winnie talks to him as though he is a developmentally delayed child who does not understand the fundamentals of human movement.

In Winnie's world, the end echoes the beginning.

What a curse, mobility!

When Eddie learned to crawl, he kept startling himself overnight by ramming his head into the cot bars. When he learned to stand, a similar thing occurred. He would wake, confused, stuck upright against the side of his cage. He rarely took long to settle back into sleep. Ivy just needed to lay him back down on the mattress, something he hadn't yet learned how to do for himself.

A month or so ago, just before Christmas, Ivy and Matt put Eddie to bed as normal. A bath with the organic milk soap, a couple of stories—he had just started pointing to objects in the books, making noises, trying to turn the thick cardboard pages—before he was zipped into his sleeping bag and put down inside his cot. The bedtime process was so consistently easy that Ivy liked to remind Matt of their luck. She told him about the arduous routines many parents had to enact each night. Sensory manipulations were needed, lighting, looped soundtracks, dummies, toys placed on precise angles in the correct corner of the room, doors left open but not too much, pats and strokes and circular rubs that were only effective when performed with the left hand, not the right, while the adult performing the gestures was in a twisted hunch beside the cot, not standing up or sitting down on the floor. By the end of the excruciating two-hour rigmarole, one mother told Ivy, I can do nothing but sit on the sofa with a glass of wine and toast my own saintliness.

That normal night, just before Christmas, Ivy listened through the baby monitor to Eddie's usual pre-sleep coos while she sent some emails. When they went to bed, they moved the baby monitor from the kitchen to their bedroom and plugged it into the power cord on Ivy's bedside table.

A few hours later, Ivy was woken by a sound she had never heard before. A shrieking, dragging sort of cry. She sat up in bed. There was a moment of silence when her fear subsided and she wondered if she had heard a sound at all. But then, there it was again, like a wounded animal, like a creature caught in a trap.

And Ivy was up and running toward Eddie. She turned on the overhead light in his bedroom as she fell through the door. In the sudden light, she squinted at her child. He was coughing but it was not a normal cough. He was crying but it was not a normal cry. He had fear and panic in his eyes, an expression Ivy had never seen in his eyes. He can't breathe, yelled Ivy. She lifted Eddie from his cot, unzipped him from his sleeping bag, undid a tiny press stud at the neck of his onesie, and held him up in front of her. Matt watched from the door. Eddie was flailing, resisting her comfort. Ivy was saying reassuring words, trying to calm her large baby, trying to breathe slowly and deeply in her own chest, channeling some vague idea that her breathing might be contagious and help him too. But he wasn't a tiny newborn still connected to his mother's body. He was a robust almost-toddler who could not breathe, a heavy human with a big round head who had been perfectly healthy at bedtime.

His lips are blue, Matt said. That's bad.

Yes. And Ivy gave Eddie to his father as she ran to their bedroom.

It was a warm night and she was only wearing underpants. She pulled on some shorts and a T-shirt, and the room seemed to coagulate around her. The air felt heavy. Her arms seemed to be pushing through a hot density, in slow motion. She had to twice put her feet inside her slip-on shoes before they settled and made sense.

The thing is happening again, Ivy thought. The worst thing is happening again, right now.

They went to the car. They put Eddie into his car seat. He had rarely been outside at night, awake, and the lights through the darkness shifted his attention away from his own fear. Ivy drove, and Eddie and Matt sat in the backseat of the car. Eddie kept making the screeching, dragging sound.

Ivy drove like a stunt driver down the long shopping strip between their house and the hospital, not stopping or slowing down once. There were no people on the roads. It was 2 a.m. It was a Tuesday. The neon lights from the shopfronts, blurring in colorful stripes outside the car, were mesmerizing and calming to their child.

At the hospital, the emergency parking bays were full and Ivy pulled into a disabled spot. She carried Eddie inside, jogging, holding her car keys. Matt followed a step behind, carrying a nappy bag he'd bundled up. Eddie's lips were bluer in the fluorescent light of the hospital, his cheeks a strange color. Those round, soft, wobbling cheeks of his. There were rows of cream laminate chairs fastened to the mauve linoleum floor. There were people filling out forms. There were children in pajamas. There were children crying. There were parents crying. There were people watching *The Love Boat* on an oversized TV attached to the wall with thick arms of black steel. There were children staring into a large bubbling aquarium, shouting at the tropical fish and seahorses inside. There were three nurses in pale green scrubs seated behind a desk.

One of the nurses looked at Ivy and looked at Eddie. She stood up and came around from behind the desk. She put her hand on Ivy's back. Her hand was warm and she smelled faintly of patchouli.

Come this way, she motioned, her dreadlocks swinging. Come right through, right away.

Then Eddie was on a hospital bed with a needle full of steroids going into his body. Ivy crouched beside him, trying not to get in the way. He was still flailing, pulling on the nurse's hand.

He's got some fight in him! the nurse laughed. I'm almost losing a thumb.

And then he gasped. And sobbed hard into his mother's shoulder. Ivy and Matt and the two nurses inside the cubicle all exhaled and resumed their own normal breathing.

It was croup, with that distinctive screeching, sliding sound. It usually occurs after a virus, but sometimes arrives without warning, in the night, and stops the breath. You did the right thing coming straight to the hospital, the nurse explained. He needed that steroid. He needed it to open the airways.

A fortnight later, once Eddie was well and Ivy was still finding it difficult to sleep, Matt said to her, Maybe you're making a bit of a mountain out of a molehill.

You think so? she said. I thought he was going to die.

I know you did. But he's a solid unit.

Yes.

You have to trust him, Matt said.

After Rupert died, Ivy thought she would never dare to have another baby. But she did, sixteen years later, with a different man, and the second time is better because the father is better and her baby did not die during infancy.

Those are her facts. But she cannot always differentiate between the two experiences. She cannot always trust, as Matt suggested.

Just as her lost child will not age, neither does her grief. The sorrow does not feel many years old. It hasn't matured or lost intensity. When she feels it, it floods her, as it always has, despite the facts, despite the years, despite the professionals, despite the improved spouse and their perfect new son.

Was I making a mountain out of a molehill, second husband? And, if so, what does that mean exactly? Was I exaggerating the scale of an experience that is similar in form to something else? Was Eddie's croup a molehill? Was Rupe's death a mountain? There was a moment when that molehill felt exactly like that mountain. The same heavy shape lodged inside my body. The same horrified awareness arrived in me and settled there.

A few weeks after Rupert died, Ivy traveled from Paris to Ussy-sur-Marne to see Beckett's house and garden. She got up one morning after barely sleeping, pulled on some clothes, and left her apartment with a bag that held only her wallet, her keys, a notebook, and a digital camera. She knew the name of the village. She would find the house when she arrived at the station.

She caught the train from Gare de Lyon and sat staring through the dirty window at the rapid views outside, the buildings of the *banlieues*, increasingly sparse, then the countryside, all of it made grayer and blurrier by insistent, very light rain. She drank from a hipflask of whiskey and had a block of four seats to herself—the window seat she settled in, the aisle seat next to her, and the pair opposite. There was a brown faux-wood table between the pairs of chairs, as though instead of drinking alone she might have been playing a magnetic board game or sharing a newspaper crossword with her fellow travelers.

She was relieved about the lack of a crowd, considering that Euro Disney was so close to her destination. Maybe there was a direct express train for the Disney people, or maybe they all traveled by coach, singing songs, wearing Mickey Mouse ears, reclining on seats with plush, cartoonish upholstery. Thank god they weren't on her train. People who chose to go to Disneyland when they were in Paris were not the people Ivy wanted on her train.

At the station in Ussy, she picked up a brochure from a pile left at an unattended information booth. *Découvrir le village de Beckett*, the brochure beckoned, with a minimalist map featuring a black star at the location of his house.

Ivy walked directly toward the black star. She smoked cigarettes and nodded at the few people she saw along the way, a farmer sitting up high inside a tractor, a woman checking her letterbox on the roadside at the end of a long, narrow driveway.

She found the house. She stood and looked at it from across the other side of the country road. A basic structure, even with its recent extension, set back from the curb. Beckett's gray cinderblock wall, an ugly solution to his quest for privacy, was less ugly than she expected because its large bricks were almost entirely obscured by dark tangles of vine. The tendrils were trimmed around a gleaming plaque announcing the house's significance as Beckett's former residence.

Ivy sat down on the verge of the road, maybe for one hour, maybe two. She looked at Beckett's trees in the breeze—high, dense conifers, elegant maples, apples and plums just starting to blossom, and citrus trees with acid-green leaves. The large stretch of lawn that he watched from his study window was smooth that day, no obvious signs of the dreaded moles that dashed across his view, ruining his idyll and his concentration.

SB liked to tend to the garden beds and fragile seedlings. He planted all those trees, investing. He removed stones from the dirt, cultivated the soil, and sowed ryegrass. He had problems with wild boars but they were transitory in their destructions, stomping through his efforts before continuing on their way. But the moles. The moles got in deep. The pockmarked grass infuriated him—those endless mounds of earth disrupting his quest for a bucolic lawn. Such torment in his sanctuary.

The moles were abundant in the village, but they were especially keen on the garden belonging to the famous writer. Neighboring children threw moles over the fence into Beckett's property, just to increase the mole population in the garden belonging to the famous writer.

The collective noun for moles is a labor, SB wrote in a letter to a friend.

A labor of moles forming craters and holes. Those swift maneuvers of pink noses and paws, and tubular velvet pelts.

Eventually, the famous writer got some Talpirid poison and threw it all over his lawn. So much for tending to the earth.

Ivy thinks about Beckett's garden as she watches Winnie on stage, her body poking up out of the ruptured ground like one of those burrowing animals. The Ussy moles might have given Beckett the visual idea for Winnie's plight. Maybe he made a mound—if not a mountain—out of a molehill, and let his imagination take off.

Ivy smiles in the dark to think of it.

One mole digging a hole.

Two snakes with garden rakes.

Three bears picking pears.

Four foxes filling boxes.

And on it goes.

Ivy knows the whole sequence by heart. It is one of Eddie's favorite books, the one with a mole pictured on the cover, wearing gumboots and wielding a spade it does not need.

The love for that book has coincided with Eddie's roaring stage, his compulsion to make the same undifferentiated noise at any nonhuman creature he encounters, both in a picture and in reality. Even if the animal is wearing a dress or driving a train in a book, he makes the same sound, that small roar, and he uses it for bears or moles or snakes, dogs at the playground, birds in a painting. Eddie always recognizes the animal as an animal, regardless of the species. He never confuses the human with the nonhuman. In his sub-two-year-old perception, a snake and a goat have more in common than a human and a goat, even a human and a gorilla.

Why does he perceive that? Is it something to do with language? Human beings speak, whereas nonhumans roar? Has he deduced that somehow? But, then, what does that categorizing mean for the preverbal infant?

Eddie's roaring is a revelation to Ivy. No wonder we have destroyed the planet, she thinks, if the tiniest people have an innate sense of human exceptionalism. What hope do we have of finding a new way of being with the other beings?

I should invest in more environmental projects, Ivy thinks, shifting in her seat, pulling at her skirt.

For the benefit of future generations.

It is the great problem of our time.

It is the only problem of our time.

Nothing else matters if the earth is dead.

Climate change is the key moral question of the age.

She hears these insistent statements and knows there is a truth to them.

I have my limits, she thinks. I'm not Bill Gates. I cannot cure malaria or prevent a pandemic. Or even plausibly pretend to do so.

Ivy read recently about a man, a young man, a man younger than herself—there's an increasingly applicable phrase—who is spending his tech billions on developing a machine that cleans up the oceans. The project hasn't yet been successful. Large components of the machine keep breaking off in misunderstood tidal currents. Older, more conservative rich people keep finding fault in the younger man's commitment. But he persists. A new prototype. A new team of engineers. A new testing zone.

What drive he has. What singularity of desire. Ivy doesn't feel capable of such boldness. She doesn't feel capable of seeing the world on that scale. She could clean up a beach, sure, but clean up an ocean? The oceans, plural? All oceans? No way. Her vision does not function so broadly, nor so particularly.

There are limits to her dreaming.

When Ivy went into her office earlier today—tag-teaming with Matt at home once she'd given Eddie some lunch—she sat at her desk in the city skyscraper and looked out to the dark mountain range at the edge of her view. By mid-afternoon, there were round clouds of smoke like storybook train gusts rising up across the range. When she left to meet Hilary, the air was full and hazy around the buildings in the surrounding streets. Everything in her view was changed, as though a fine mesh curtain had been pulled over the glass.

Ivy does not know if the bushfires have now been contained or if they have become horrifying and large-scale. If they have become horrifying and large-scale, Ivy knows that they will generate a rush of donations that will ensure every other charity in the country will flounder for funds for a time. This immediate and explicit horror will draw so much money away from all the other injustices that were happening before the event, that will keep happening afterward.

The world is a swarm of need, and Ivy knows she cannot save it.

I made my choices, she thinks. Children's health. Indigenous rights. Visual art. Theater. That's my bit.

There's little point fighting against what she loves, or pretending to be a different sort of visionary person. All she can do is committedly chip away at the sectors she chose, years ago.

She won't get stuck in deriding herself for caring about the wrong things, for thinking if only she made different decisions then the planet would be fixed. Fuck that. It wouldn't be. She doesn't have a god complex. She is not delusional about the extent of her own power.

There is a research center for pediatric respiratory health in Adelaide, established a few years ago with a grant from Ivy's foundation. It was suggested that the center should be named in her honor. She rebuffed the idea, as she has rebuffed any similar suggestion. She is not a typical philanthropist. She doesn't want a building named after her or even a sparkling function room off a mirror-lined corridor. The Ivy Parker Center for Pediatric Respiratory Research. The Parker Anteroom. No, not that. She has been considered uncooperative in her determination not to allow her name to be chiseled into gold. She will not provide a studio photograph of herself to be stuck on a wall alongside an extended label detailing her generosity. She has declined two invitations to be the subject of an Archibald Prize portrait, even though one of the painters collaborated on a limited-edition clothing range with her favorite designer and would have depicted her with a tempting, heightened glamour.

It is only recently that Ivy has even been recognized as the important person waiting for the meeting. For many years, it was assumed she was the important person's pretty young assistant, that there was an old man in a suit nearby who had just popped out for a piss.

She doesn't think of the money as her fortune, just the fortune. She gives herself a reasonable salary and generous salaries to her staff (currently two full-time assistants and a part-time marketing person, although the part-time marketing person suggested she should soon consider hiring a dedicated social media professional). The rest is the fortune. She has to invest portions of the fortune and she has to release portions of it to other people and organizations.

It is her life's work and her life's great puzzle—an administrative, mathematical, ethical puzzle. She would be embarrassed to be celebrated for simply opening the box that was given to her and sorting through the pieces inside.

On stage, Winnie has returned to inspecting her toothbrush.

Genuine pure . . . fully guaranteed . . . hog . . . What exactly is a hog, Willie, do you know?

Castrated male swine. Reared for slaughter.

Winnie's smile stretches wide across her face in the bright light.

The first act is almost over. It will soon be intermission.

Ivy needs to get into the right headspace for talking to people, networking, bridging, all the bullshit. There will be several people from the theater company with oblique job titles. She hopes that one day, in a conversation about money, someone might define themselves without euphemism. I'm the Fundraiser for the Organization, they'll say. I'm the Head Money Seeker. More likely, yet another employee will shake her hand and declare himself to be the Relationships Officer. The Stakeholder Liaison Manager. The Development Director. The co-opting of development when referring to finances is Ivy's particular gripe.

To cut through the palaver, Ivy might say—I'm Ivy Parker,

Woman with Money. The people wanting her money will laugh, of course, because they are obliged to do so.

To finish with a prayer or a song? On stage, that is the present question. Winnie is unsure of the most appropriate way to complete her day.

Would a prayer emphasize her need? Would a song emphasize her gratitude? Or would the reverse be true? Should she sing a song of yearning, or say a prayer of appreciation?

Go with the song every time, Ivy thinks. Choose the song.

Sing your song, Winnie.

No? Then pray.

Pray your prayer, Winnie.

Winnie bows her head.

And it is intermission.

The
Intermission

CHARACTERS

SUMMER
female, early 20s, theater usher

PROFESSOR MARGOT PIERCE
female, early 70s, audience member

IVY PARKER
female, early 40s, audience member

HILARY FULLER
female, early 40s, audience member

JOEL
male, mid-20s, audience member

APRIL
female, mid-20s (screen and voice only)

SCENE 1

....

A mirror-lined passage. Bright purple floor carpet. Row of rose-gold sconce lights, fractal shaped, along top of mirrors.

At stage left, corridor ends with swing door—Staff Only. At right, corridor extends offstage toward unseen main foyer and bar area.

Along passage, two bench seats upholstered in multicolored striped velvet.

SUMMER sits on bench seat, head in hands.

SUMMER stands and walks to Staff Only *door as though about to enter. She pauses, turns around, and assumes a position of authority at center stage.*

MARGOT enters from stage right.

MARGOT: Preordered drinks?

PAUSE

MARGOT: Where are the preordered drinks?

SUMMER: Sorry. They're on the end of the bar in the main foyer.

MARGOT: Same as always. I knew that.

MARGOT heads to the bar, going back the way she came.

SUMMER: (*calling after MARGOT*) Right-hand side.

MARGOT: (*calling back to SUMMER*) Thank you!

PAUSE

MARGOT reappears with a full champagne flute. There is a paper receipt stuck to bottom of glass. She picks it off, shakes it free from her fingers. Receipt floats to carpet.

MARGOT: I got out of there quickly. Like to get a head start.

SUMMER: Won't be long.

MARGOT sits on bench seat at stage left, sips drink.

SUMMER: I enjoyed your lecture in Eco Lit last semester.

MARGOT: (*startled, looking at SUMMER*) I always remember my students and you're—

SUMMER: It was just the one lecture and—

MARGOT: Of course, guest lecture. *North and South*?

SUMMER nods.

MARGOT: Like it?

SUMMER: Yeah. I liked all the books in that subject. It was really interesting. I'm not a literature—

MARGOT: I'm not a Gaskell fan. She's overwrought.

> *During the above exchange, increasing sounds of a human crowd, as well as noise from bar—glasses clinking, etc.*

> *IVY and HILARY enter from stage right. IVY spots empty bench seat, sits down, and pulls out phone. HILARY sits beside her. They lean together, both peering at IVY's phone.*

IVY: (*gesturing to phone photo*) I might be a tad biased, but just look at the state of him.

HILARY: Nah. What is that hat? He's objectively adorable—

MARGOT: Ivy Parker!

PAUSE

IVY: (*seeing MARGOT*) Oh my god.

> *MARGOT and IVY stand in front of bench seats, then rush to embrace. MARGOT spills some champagne down IVY's back.*

IVY: I can't believe it.

MARGOT: I thought you were dead.

IVY: (*pulling away from MARGOT*) You did not.

MARGOT: You're as exquisite as ever, darling girl. How can you look like that after, what, almost twenty years? My god.

IVY: Must be the sleep deprivation.

MARGOT: Children?

IVY: Just the one. But he sleeps fine. (*IVY places her hand on HILARY's waist, guides her toward MARGOT*) I'm here with Hilary. Hilary Fuller. She has three children. And she's a writer.

MARGOT: (*shaking hands with HILARY*) Of course. It was the three of you in a row in all my lectures. You two, and that sweetheart of a boy? (*twisting her head to speak to SUMMER*) I told you I remember my students.

> *SUMMER nods. She is pacing around the space. During the scene, SUMMER exits through* Staff Only *door at stage left, and returns, repeatedly.*

IVY: Matt. The sweetheart.

HILARY: Professor, she married him.

MARGOT: You married your friend from uni? I expected more, Ivy. I thought you'd do fascinating things.

> *MARGOT takes a large gulp of her champagne. Glass is now empty.*

IVY: It's okay, Prof. (*IVY pats MARGOT on the arm in consolation*) He's my second husband. Things have happened.

MARGOT: Ha! (*to HILARY*) What kind of writer are you?

HILARY: Oh. Lifestyle stuff. Interiors. Bit of food, travel.

MARGOT: Fun?

HILARY: Well, I'm an expert on cushion piping this week.

IVY: (*to MARGOT*) We're meant to be going to a drinks reception. You can come, if you'd like?

MARGOT: Sure. Thanks.

IVY links her elbows with HILARY and MARGOT, one woman on either side of her. They head toward function room, a bit follow-the-yellow-brick-road.

SUMMER, jittery, remains standing near Staff Only *door.*

MARGOT: So what're the drinks for?

IVY: I'm giving a grant to the theater company to expand their female directors program. They think they're still wooing me.

MARGOT stops walking, pulls IVY and HILARY to a standstill.

MARGOT: You give grants? You have serious money?

IVY: (*laughing*) I run the Parker Foundation. We're focused on—

MARGOT is now almost slapstick in her expression of shock.

MARGOT: You're the Parker Foundation? I know some of the work you do! My god. My brilliant underprivileged scholarship girl. I bought your books for you in third year.

IVY: Did you? I didn't know that was you.

MARGOT: Ha! Sorry. Yes. Yes, that was—

IVY: Thank you. We should get to the drinks. I hate being late. I'm going to have to talk to a lot of people.

HILARY: She's still as conchie as ever.

MARGOT: I'm shocked. Thrilled, but—

HILARY: I bet.

MARGOT: —shocked. Can you give me a brief summary? I don't think I can get through the intermission without knowing. Where did this money come from? (*smiling*) Was it the first husband?

IVY: (*shaking her head, laughing*) No, no. Nanna died during my final year at uni—

MARGOT: Yes, I remember that.

IVY: —and I sold all her stuff. Nothing major. No car. House belonged to the government. Just trinkets. Mostly junk but, you know, it adds up. I had enough to buy a backpack and an airfare to Paris.

MARGOT: (*delighted*) You were always a Francophile. Didn't you do your honors thesis on French lit?

IVY: (*a bit mortified*) It was Duras and Beckett. Dialogue in the fiction of Duras and Beckett.

MARGOT: Very impressive.

IVY: (*shaking her head*) Not really. I only wrote about them from the English. I didn't work in the French. Anyway.

HILARY: Anyway. I was in Europe too then. Great times.

IVY: And my mum's friends from college—

MARGOT: Your parents died when you were a baby. I remember—

IVY: Toddler. Yeah. Mum's friends lived in London, took me in when I got overseas, looked after me, loved me—

MARGOT: In a hot-air balloon?

IVY: What?

MARGOT: Your parents died in a hot-air balloon?

HILARY: No. Light plane. They won the flight in a competition. They almost took Ivy with them but she was too little. Wasn't allowed.

IVY: Yep. Anyway. We have to go to the drinks.

MARGOT: Hang on. Your mum's friends?

IVY: Rich. Old money. I hadn't realized quite the extent of it. They left me their money. No kids of their own. That's it. They hoped I'd do something interesting with it. I'm still working it out, years later.

> MARGOT shakes her head, incredulous. IVY is impatient.

HILARY: It's good, isn't it?

MARGOT: It's straight out of a nineteenth-century novel. An orphan with a fortune! Oh my lord.

> *IVY rolls her eyes and pulls the other two women to start walking again.*
>
> *IVY, MARGOT, and HILARY exit toward function room.*
>
> *SUMMER exits through* Staff Only *door.*

SCENE 2

A small staffroom. Lockers line two side walls. Back wall is mirrored above waist height and painted bright purple to floor. Gray vinyl ottoman in center of the space. Well lit. Quiet.

Above room, a large display screen, showing a phone's home screen. The phone belongs to SUMMER. A photograph of SUMMER and APRIL on screen, mostly obscured by a series of message notifications. The sender of the messages is APRIL. The contents of the messages are not shown.

SUMMER jogs into staffroom. She attempts to open combination lock. She gets combination wrong and begins again.

SUMMER: Fuck, fuck, fuck, fuck.

SUMMER opens locker. She pulls out a backpack and finds her phone.

SUMMER sits on ottoman. She opens the three waiting messages, one after another. The contents of the messages are visible on display screen.

APRIL: (*text message*) Wind change. Getting sketchy up there x

APRIL: (*text message*) FYI, I'm going to drive up and meet them halfway. Woolf is cray cray, poor baby x

APRIL: (*text message*) Traffic shite. I love you, Sum. Things a bit scary

> *SUMMER stands. She is calling APRIL.*
>
> *A photo of APRIL appears on display screen as phone dials. In photo, APRIL has short peroxide-blonde hair with dark roots, dark lipstick, big smile, tattoos on pale décolletage.*
>
> *Image on screen flutters off to momentary black. APRIL answers. On screen, APRIL is frowning. Her face is red and shiny.*

APRIL: I had to pull over. They're not letting us go up. Just then. Like I've just—

SUMMER: Where are you?

APRIL: —pulled over this second. Near Maxi Foods. The smoke is intense. I just wanted to be here. The thought of them up there—

> *Image on display screen wobbles away from APRIL's face. A large, floodlit supermarket. A car park. Smoke haze. Dark shape of a looming mountain range.*

APRIL: (*voice audible over images on screen*) —in there, just right there. What if they can't do it the way they have before? The smoke is so full-on. It's so hot, like fucking crazy hot, and it's what, eight? Nine? It shouldn't be this hot. It's fucking apocalyptic.

SUMMER: What are you doing, Ape? Aren't you getting in the way? They'll drive out if—

APRIL: They can't drive out.

PAUSE

APRIL's face on display screen. She is outside, next to car. APRIL is holding phone unsteadily. She is not looking at phone. Edge of APRIL's face intermittently visible on screen. Mainly car park and smoke haze.

In staffroom, SUMMER is standing still, staring at phone in hand.

APRIL: There is no way they can drive out. The roads are blocked. I mean, unless they're in the cars still coming out now. They would've told me if they were going to leave. Surely. It's too late. We fucked up. We just—

SUMMER: Don't get any closer. You're too close.

APRIL: —fucked up. There are embers down here. Like, just every now and then, a flaming thing will float past. Look.

APRIL moves phone to capture embers on screen. A brief flash of light across bitumen ground. Another longer flash—a spark rolling and lengthening across black.

SUMMER grimaces at phone. She looks away.

APRIL: It doesn't even make sense. The wind is all over the place. Aren't you still at work?

SUMMER: (*holding phone close to mouth now, no longer looking at it*) It's intermission. I've come down to the locker room. I shouldn't be down here. I couldn't stand it. I've been so anxious. For the whole first act, I've been trying to keep my shit together. I'm so sorry.

> *At the start of the above speech, phones disconnect. On display screen, view of APRIL at car park flashes to black, replaced by home screen of SUMMER's phone with happy couple photo of SUMMER and APRIL, visible now that messages have gone. In photo, SUMMER has small flowers threaded through her long dark hair, glitter eye shadow, tipsy smile. APRIL, with bright red lips, is kissing her cheek.*

SUMMER: I'm so worried about you. I did some good breathing. I got out. I love your mum and dad but I don't want you to help them. I just want you to be okay. I love you, Ape. Maybe you could just get back in the car and drive back to— Oh fuck. No. You've gone. How long have you been gone?

> *SUMMER slumps onto ottoman.*

> *PAUSE*

> *SUMMER fiddles with phone. She is on the emergency services app. She is scrolling through fire warnings, watch-and-act warnings, evacuation instructions, notification options, etc. She is zooming in and out on maps, tapping, sliding.*

There are red exclamation marks all over maps. There are orange triangles. There are shaded areas of black. There are shaded areas of red. There are i's in italics for information. There are town names in fonts of various sizes.

All this written and graphic information on display screen, in flashes.

APRIL's photo face appears on display screen as SUMMER's phone rings. Voice call this time.

APRIL: (*voice only*) They just called. They've got the next-door neighbors with them. The four of them are doing prep stuff. Their son is actually at the theater, they think. Your theater. They haven't been able to get in touch with him. His phone always runs out of—

SUMMER: I can find him.

APRIL: He's got a parrot tatt on his arm. Bicep. I did it. He's my age, bit cute. Studying secondary ed, I think. Ginger. Joel.

SUMMER: Like a native parrot? Like a cockatoo or a rosella or—

APRIL: King parrot. Red. Green. Macho as fuck. We used to feed them when we were kids. He's got a full sleeve on one arm. The parrot's on its own on the other—

SUMMER: Have I met this guy?

APRIL: Dunno. He lives somewhere annoying now, I can't remember. Maybe he was at home over Easter when we were up here? You might have met his parents. They're lovely. Two older sisters. Maybe?

SUMMER: Don't think so. Joel. Okay. I'll find him—

Display screen blackens.

SUMMER: —and then should I just tell him to call his mum? Are you just going to stay where—

PAUSE

SUMMER looks at phone in her hand.

SUMMER: Oh fuck. You've gone again. Okay.

SUMMER picks up backpack and throws it into locker. She puts her phone inside locker on top of bag. Locks locker.

SUMMER looks at her reflection in mirror. She tries some different faces in mirror, all a version of professional or composed. She exits.

PAUSE

SUMMER reenters staffroom. She unlocks combination lock, opens locker, pulls out phone, shoves it into her pocket, relocks locker, exits.

SCENE 3

. . . .

Mirrored passage, as before.

There is a pretty chime sounding, marking the end of intermission.

SUMMER enters through Staff Only *door. She looks at herself in mirror.*

SUMMER walks toward stage right, leaning over to pick up three discarded ice-cream sticks. She looks around for a rubbish bin, puts ice-cream sticks into her trouser pocket.

SUMMER pulls phone from other pocket, looks at it.

IVY enters from stage right.

SUMMER slides phone inside trouser pocket, nods politely at IVY.

IVY: Hello.

SUMMER: The second act's about to start.

IVY: I know. There's always a bit of time after the chime.

SUMMER: Yeah.

IVY: It was busy in there. At the drinks function.

SUMMER: (*nodding*) Sometimes I work them. They can get quite crowded.

IVY: How bad are those bloody heavy white platters? Can't believe they're still standard.

SUMMER: (*surprised, smiling*) Those platters are the worst.

IVY: Total wrist breakers.

IVY and SUMMER smile in agreement.

IVY: And circle breakers too. That's actually what I used to call them when I worked functions. You really have to push those platters into the conversation circles.

SUMMER: (*laughing*) Totally. Although it's worse when you can't break in, and you're standing there nudging someone's back—

IVY: —with the edge of the thing, being ignored.

SUMMER: Totally.

IVY: And if you do break in, they either dive on the hors d'oeuvres like they're starving, or just look pissed off for being interrupted.

SUMMER: Or they ask a dumb question about ingredients. Like, what's that tomato-and-mozzarella bruschetta got in it? Any meat?

IVY laughs.

SUMMER notices piece of paper on carpet. It is MARGOT's drink receipt. SUMMER picks up paper, scrunches it, shoves it into trouser pocket.

PAUSE

SUMMER: The second act is about to start.

IVY: I was just curious about the art in the function room. The waiter in there couldn't tell me much, but maybe you know more about it? The big triptych opposite the mirrored wall?

SUMMER: Oh. Our training's not that comprehensive, sorry.

IVY: No. But it's Indigenous?

PAUSE

IVY: I just thought you might—

SUMMER: (*stiffening*) You need to head back inside, madam. The second act really is about to start. Sorry.

The pretty chime sounds again.

IVY: Okay. Thank you. Thanks anyway.

IVY exits stage right.

SUMMER pulls phone out of pocket, checks it.

SUMMER: (*exiting in a rush*) Ginger. Tattoo. Joel. Yep. Joel.

SCENE 4

....

Staffroom, as before. Blank display screen above room.

SUMMER and JOEL enter staffroom.

SUMMER opens locker, pulls out phone charger from backpack, plugs it into power point at base of mirrored wall.

SUMMER: There you go.

JOEL puts charger into his phone.

Display screen lights up with the home screen of JOEL's phone. Photograph of a dense mountain ash forest taken from ground, looking up—tall trees reaching to blue cloudless sky. Photograph of trees is covered by several message notifications.

JOEL: (*sitting on ottoman, staring at phone*) Oh shit.

SUMMER: (*squatting down next to ottoman*) It's not a good situation.

Lights out. End.

Seven

The lights flash on over the stage and Margot's throat catches at the sight of Winnie. She is buried up to her neck now. Only her head and the black feathered hat on top of her hair remain outside of the mound. Her eyes are closed.

Oh, this is horrific. Margot shifts in her chair. She has not seen this before. She thought she had seen the play but she has not seen this.

Did she leave at intermission the last time she saw the play all those years ago in that small studio theater down the side street? It's possible. She was pregnant. The seats were uncomfortable. Perhaps she did not endure beyond the first act.

This sight of Winnie, almost entirely consumed by the earth, is nowhere to be found in Margot's memory.

Bzzzzzzzz! That wretched bell!

Winnie's eyes snap open. *Hail, holy light.*

Winnie's eyes close.

Bzzzzzzzz! The bell, again!

Winnie's eyes snap open.

It seems the poor consumed woman is now to be denied any rest. Surely she was suffering enough without adding that nasty variable to her lot. What torture this is to witness.

Eyes on my eyes. Winnie blinks and Winnie smiles—an odd, puppet-y smile, as though the two sides of her mouth are being hooked back by a mechanism behind her neck, her lips stretched straight and wide.

May one still speak of time?

Of course, Winnie. Is there anything else to speak of?

It's very troubling to consider how time has acted on Winnie in her mound. Margot wants to ask her so many questions.

How long has it taken for the earth to rise over you, for the hot dirt to reach your jaw? Or is it you who has moved through time and space? Have you sunk down? The mound looks rigid from up here in the dark but maybe it is malleable. Has the earth found room to absorb you? Is your flesh succumbing to microbes and rot and all that deathly business? Are you—how can I express it delicately—composting?

Oh, this is horrific. Margot is unsure if she is going to be able to keep looking at this for long. She wasn't expecting such a scene after intermission. She just wanted to come back into the theater, sit down, and think. As she settled into her chair, she made a mental list of the people she would contemplate during the second act of the play.

Ivy Parker.

Hilary Fuller.

Adam, Grace, and baby Lily.

She would not waste the opportunity for some forced thinking time. She would use it to consider those people.

But then—this. A head stuck in the earth, talking.

She's an actress, you silly woman, Margot scolds herself. You don't need to be worried about her dying body. Only a twit would conflate a theatrical performance with material reality, or allow oneself to be emotionally manipulated by Samuel Beckett, that productive nihilist. I mean, come on, Professor. Get a grip.

How pleasant it is to have this armrest to myself, Margot thinks.

The young man seated beside her during the first act of the play has not returned for the second. She noticed him at the top of the stairs when the chime was sounding to mark the end of intermission, as she was coming back inside with Hilary Fuller. But the young man did not make it to his seat from the stairs. Curious.

He probably lost his nerve at the final hurdle. Couldn't bear the thought of another minute of being forced to watch a woman rabbiting on about her existence. He would have been bored, at any rate, and concentration spans are not what they used to be. All that rapid cognitive processing over tiny screens. He's probably gone off to a pirate bar with his pirate tattoo to drink a macho pirate-y drink. He's probably listening to one of those cunning true-crime podcasts or sending dick pics on Tinder. I know the type. Good riddance, young man. I thought you were quite rude.

Margot crosses her legs toward the empty seat and hangs her elbow over the available armrest. The air conditioning is prickly on her skin. She will be very cold by the time the play is over. Can it really be stifling hot outside, with bushfires raging into the night? Can it really be over forty degrees? In here, it'd be half that. If that. It's impossible to dress for this horrid weather.

She should have put a wrap inside her handbag. She always remembers to pop a wrap into her handbag when she goes to the cinema a couple of times each year. She's been known to drape her scarf across her own knees and the knees of her companion, a friend or John, both of them laughing in the dark about Margot's sensitivity and Margot's preparedness. Tonight, there is no preparedness, only sensitivity.

She must be feeling colder than the other people here. She must be feeling particularly cold. There is no way the thermostat would be set so low on purpose, so that all of us are frigid. She cannot conjure an economic or social reason why the place would be made deliberately cold. Overheated, sure, so then everyone would be thirstier at intermission and spend more money on drinks, but cold, no, there's no plausible rationale.

On stage, Winnie is struggling to understand what she has become.

My arms. My breasts. What arms? What breasts?

Her body is missing—buried? destroyed?—and she is concerned that she no longer exists at all.

What horror it would be if only the mind remained—to be left with one's incessant cognitions without the solace of the corporeal.

Margot crosses her own arms over her own breasts as though to reassure herself that she can do so. She rubs her palms over her soft, cold biceps. She scratches a mosquito bite she finds there, her nail going over and across the bite several times. She slides her hands toward her elbows and feels a quick tenderness as her fingers pass a bruise. That's the old, green one, she remembers. Neatly circular, like a cartoon planet.

Margot often wallows in the visual aesthetics of her bruises, looking at them with a neutral detachment. She likes to consider the possibility that her body is making a sort of art from the shame of being hurt.

Margot remembers the bruise stories she would tell herself as a child. She would choose a leg, for example, and examine each bruise on it, and write the story of how it appeared.

A charcoal gray stripe from running into the telephone table in the hall.

A large yellow blotch from kneeling hard on a pile of jacks.

A jagged red skyline of marks—replete with a storm-cloud bruise behind—after smashing her shin on a fence.

After she saw her uncles, Margot would have extra stories to recount to her bruise diary. The dark bruises above her kneecap from the horse bites. The small ones on the tops of her thighs like the fingerprints of a crime suspect made from faint purple ink, pressed down onto her flesh in a row.

The worst uncle didn't usually leave bruises, until the time that he did.

Margot thinks of him—his sheen of sweat, the broken capillaries across his cheeks and nose, his beery smell, his smooth cream hands.

She coughs, shifts her body in the theater dark, and pulls the memory forward.

At Christmas, Easter, big birthdays, Melbourne Cup, all the uncles and aunties and cousins would gather at a house. The families would take turns to host, to share the load of providing enough beer and food. There could never be too much beer and food. The houses were interchangeable. The gatherings were the same, wherever they were. The aunties were always in the kitchen with the food, often talking about bodily pains that Margot did not yet understand. The ladies seemed so pleased to be together in the kitchen. Margot's mother grew calmer in the company of the other women, as if the chance to cook and talk with them was a relief or a release. A relieving release, was that it?

When Margot was too little to help with the food preparation, she understood she shouldn't be in the kitchen. If she went in there, the women would stop talking and smile tensely at her and ask her what she wanted. Nothing, she would answer. Just came in to say hello. Well, hello, Margot, a few of them might reply, until she skipped back out to where she belonged, which was roaming around the house and the yard and the street with the cousins.

But the cousins didn't like me much, Margot thinks. Too big for my boots. Too smart. Too uppity. It wasn't always the best idea to play with the cousins unless she wanted to have her plaits pulled out or her dress smeared with mud, and even when she tried to join in and not annoy them, something bad would still happen, like she'd get left halfway up a tree or scrunched in a wardrobe for hours because no one could be bothered to search for her in their game of hide-and-seek.

The uncles would sit in a circle in the lounge room on easy chairs and a couple of other chairs dragged from around the kitchen table because the women never sat down, not at all, until the end of the whole long day. If it was warm, the men would sit in a circle outside on stools just large enough to handle their bulk.

Margot was the most popular girl with the uncles. They used to fight to be the first man to pull her from standing and drag her onto their laps. I've got you first, Marg! Come here, love. It's my turn. And she would settle herself where she was plonked and wait for the pinches on her thighs, the horse bites above her knees, the pony rides that started in a slow trot and accelerated into a squealing gallop and were sometimes exhilarating—like the best tickle—and sometimes a frightening and blurry struggle with Margot falling in a heap on the carpet or the grass at an uncle's feet.

The worst uncle was quieter. He would wait until the rest of them were getting another bottle of beer or piling more food onto their plates, and then he'd hoick Margot onto him and slide his hand between her thighs and under the thin pale fabric of her underpants. He'd frantically flap his fingers around in there. Oh, you are so soft, he'd moan. So, so soft. His flushed cheeks would get redder and his beery pant would get fast against her face.

One Easter, Margot walked in on the worst uncle in the bathroom. He was not sitting on the toilet. He was straddling the rim of the bath, one shoed foot inside the tub, the other on a pale green bathmat. His trousers were still zipped up but his button-down shirt was untucked. A strange purplish knob was sticking out of the top of his waistband. It was a smooth, moist dome, like a peeled plum, and he was rubbing it with his frantic flapping fingers. Margot stood in the doorway and watched, and she could not understand what she was looking at. It was only years later, when she saw another erect penis, that she realized it could go all the way up there. Straight up. So up that it could sit right out of the waistband of a pair of trousers. And so when the worst uncle told her to kiss the strange knob, she sneered at him in horror, not because she didn't want to put her mouth on an erect penis but because she didn't want to put her mouth on the worst uncle. He reached out, grabbed her arm—whisper-hissed into her face—and threw her across the tiled floor. Her body came to a stop against the toilet. She raised her head and squeezed her eyes shut against the sight of him still straddling the edge of the bathtub. Later, she tallied up her bruise diary. One cheek bruise.

Two arm bruises. She told her mother that she'd fallen out of the liquidambar in the backyard.

Tonight, for the first time since the problems with John began, someone asked Margot about the marks on her body.

What happened there? Ivy Parker was matter-of-fact, open to any answer she might receive.

Hearing Ivy pose the question, Margot wondered again why it had never been asked. Is it that no one has noticed, or is it that no one has wanted to intrude? Or is it inconceivable that the inimitable Professor Pierce could be subject to violence? Or perhaps bruises on old ladies aren't notable. We become less absorbent as we age, of course. Our flesh is a poorer sponge, unable to disperse the blows.

Margot appreciates that strangers might not feel comfortable talking about the bruises—even if they notice them—but she has waited months for one of her friends, or her colleagues, or her neighbors, or her son, or her daughter-in-law, or anyone else to ask her something. How extraordinary that it took Ivy Parker, beloved prodigal student, to say the words.

They were mid-cheers inside the function room, champagne flutes aloft, delighted in their rediscovery of one another after two decades.

Ouch, Ivy said. What happened there?

Margot's eyes jumped to her own arm to confirm what Ivy was seeing.

She noted the bruise that resembled an attempted lake in an amateur watercolor—a large mess of browns and blues—and another cluster of small red dots. Margot doesn't know enough about the vascular system to understand why those small red dots have formed. Will they join together and change hue? Do the dots signify deep damage, or the opposite—a superficial harm on the surface? Who knows? But there the bruises were, on Margot's bare arm in her shift dress, exposed and rainbowed in the intense halogen glare of the function room.

Oh, yes, they're quite something in this light, Margot joked. Just a garden injury.

Climbing trees? Ivy smiled.

Well, almost, Margot said. I got a bit high up with the loppers and took a tumble. I tend to over-prune. A controlling instinct, no doubt.

Someone from the theater company intervened then, pulling Ivy away.

How on earth did I come up with that? Margot thinks. And did she believe me? Good grief. Loppers? Pruning? Ivy cannot have been convinced.

Bzzzzzzzz! The bell again! Winnie's eyes, only closed for a moment, snap open.

No, no.

She smiles her wide, puppetlike grimace, punctuating her wakefulness. Her body—what remains of it—clearly wants to sleep, but the greater imperative is to remain conscious, to use her voice, to keep existing.

Margot also jolts at the piercing sound. I was saved by the bell, she thinks. It's time to redirect my train of thought. I don't want to think about what Ivy believes or what might have been said if that conversation had continued. I might have rambled about tree pruning. I might very well have detailed a complex system of seasonal branch management that resulted in sharp, sawn-off sections that are very dangerous to aging gardeners. Perhaps Ivy might have questioned me, or just raised an eyebrow to indicate she wasn't buying it. Did I imagine a momentary frown on her face as she was dragged away by the—what was he called?—the Stakeholder Relationships Officer? Enough.

Back to the list.

Hilary.

Adam.

Grace.

Lily.

It's time to activate some mental discipline, Professor, and focus on the list. You can do it.

Margot's capacity to compartmentalize has been so regularly praised that she now believes it to be one of her finest qualities. At the very least, it's allowed her to maintain a career in an environment that is riddled with dissatisfied and highly articulate people whose concerns are prima facie rather distracting. Just this afternoon, during her meeting with the dean, Margot was asked how she felt about the casual academic staff protesting against their work conditions. She shrugged. What about the bullying accusations in chancellery? She shrugged again.

Earlier in the day, she found employment for an international student whose family in Iran had made it clear they did not want her to return home with her newly minted PhD. She locked in twelve colleagues to present in a literary seminar series, a process that entailed over a hundred emails. She rated forty-eight job applications for an entry-level, part-time, contract position in her department, and had a telephone conversation with a young man who worked in central timetabling who was almost in tears about how the endless building work on campus made it impossible to solve the problem of where to put everyone each day. Margot's regular barista casually mentioned while handing over her coffee that his wife had been diagnosed with breast cancer at the age of thirty-three. A woman she didn't know asked her for a Band-Aid and some paracetamol in the ladies, and then started to talk about menopause. The professor in the office next to Margot's came into her space several times to express his horror at plans to relocate the departmental reference library. Yet another rat was seen in a corridor. She wrung out twelve hundred words on an overdue article she'd only agreed to write because it was commissioned by a website run by one of Adam's old schoolmates and it'd boost her public engagement points. The building manager sent a group email advising staff to turn off their air conditioning units because the system was overloaded due to extreme heat. She devoted a solid half hour to tweaking a guest lecture she was to deliver at the end of the week in a subject run by a colleague she pretended to like but thought was a misogynistic and entitled bore. She forgot to have lunch. She only had the one coffee because she was unsure what to say to the barista so didn't want to return to her normal coffee stand and didn't want to risk disloyalty if seen elsewhere. She made a series of appointments with John's specialist. The medical receptionist repeatedly called her Margaret and told her no appointment times were available before finding that indeed all the appointment times were available. She processed two Special Consideration requests from undergraduate students—both related to ongoing mental health conditions. She was asked to write a reference for a former graduate student who had never impressed her. She was asked to go out for dinner with a couple of old friends, one of whom scolded her for failing to be more socially proactive. She was asked to sit on an academic integrity board. She was asked to be the headline speaker at a Victorian studies conference in Venice next year. Her office wi-fi dropped out inexplicably for much of the morning.

I cannot take on every issue, Margot answered the dean. There is always one drama or another. I try to stay focused on my work.

What an enviable ability that is, the dean patronized. What extraordinary mental discipline.

Oh yes, Margot thought, so enviable. And it's emotional, rather than mental, discipline. I will not allow myself to be consumed by bad feelings wrought by bad thoughts. I've got too much to do. In the same way, if I didn't have the knack for slotting bad thoughts at the back of my mind file, I'd spend my days fretting about John's illness and his violence, and Adam's disdain.

Margot didn't verbalize the correction. She would let the dean think what he liked about her. She accepted his misguided compliment and smiled her capable smile.

On stage, Winnie's lips have unhooked from her smile, and she is looking grave. *Do you think the earth has lost its atmosphere?*

Where did that come from, Winnie? Since when have you been talking about the earth and its atmosphere? Please don't start on that. Not the bloody state of the planet. I will not listen, Margot thinks. I cannot listen.

Mental discipline, Professor. Back to the list.

She will start with Hilary. She suspects that going over her conversation with Hilary will lead to Adam and Grace and Lily. A seed of understanding is niggling at Margot like the beginning of a research question before unrelated ideas suddenly become connected and affirming. If she follows this feeling of discomfort about Hilary, perhaps she will reach some clarity about what is going on with her son and his family.

It was mid-intermission and Ivy was working the room in her philanthropic persona. Margot and Hilary were together, free champagne flowing, both of them politely conversational.

Hilary checked her phone, apologizing to Margot for being rude. I just have to see how things are going with Mum and the kids, she said.

You have one of those dream grandmothers, do you? Margot asked, with levity.

Hilary bristled.

Your mum is a keen grandmother? Margot tried again.

Sort of, Hilary said. Not particularly. This is the first time she's ever babysat for us at night—my husband has a work thing—and she made a big deal out of it, as if sitting on my couch for a few hours watching TV is infinitely more difficult than sitting on her own.

I see, Margot smiled. We still have our own lives, you know!

Do you have grandchildren? Hilary asked.

Yes. Lily. My son's baby. Her mother is a total natural so I've not been needed much, thank god.

A natural? Hilary repeated. How lovely.

They moved on—comments were made about the food and Ivy's charm on display on the other side of the room. Hilary was interested in discussing the consistency of the tart pastry; there were a couple of unruly crumbs stuck to her fingers. Margot complimented the champagne. They talked briefly about Winnie, Willie, and the light over the play. Their awkwardness diminished with the light. They were companionable and smooth, the prickles buffed away, by the time they returned together to the theater, waving goodbye as they shuffled into their rows. Ivy Parker lagged behind in the foyer to ask the usher a question.

But the baby conversation troubled Margot. Her every word seemed wrong now—loaded with meaning and cloying, indirect but seemingly candid. What were you going on about, Professor? Why comment on Hilary's babysitting situation? Why perpetuate some pat notion of the super-grandma? And natural? Grace is a natural. What clichéd waffle is that?

I didn't like being with Adam when he was a baby, Margot

thinks. I tried to like it but I did not. I was in disguise. I pushed his pram around our concrete neighborhood and wished I were carrying a placard that announced me as the person I was before. BC, Before Child. Oh, how I enjoyed that joke. If I saw groups of women with babies, I felt a deep ambivalence. I wanted to join their posse and ask them—how? How do you do this correctly? What am I doing wrong? Or, more precisely, what cognitive dissonance do I need to allow myself to enjoy this experience at this time? But when I saw a crowd of women and children, I also wanted to speed up, bouncing the pram over bluestone and across roads, as though to escape any inkling of an association with the group, scared of a contagion of contentment that was only possible with a profound letting-go into fate and circumstance.

I could not accept my fate. I fought against my circumstances. I eventually manufactured demands from my employer that meant it was essential to leave Adam with babysitters. I told lies about what people at the university were expecting of me. I complained about the fact that women's lib had barely tickled the edge of the real lives of mothers with careers.

There's so much talk of equality, I'd say, but the only way to get on with a job is to behave like a man and cast the offspring aside.

On stage, Winnie is naming facial features, as if confirming the existence of the remaining parts of herself. *The face. The nose . . . the nostrils . . . a hint of lip . . . the tongue . . . eyebrow . . . cheek.*

That's just the sort of thing I did with Adam when his speech was developing, Margot thinks. We even had a puzzle where you could take each body part away and reinstate it, over and over. Or was that a Mr. Potato Head toy? Yes. Strange-looking thing. And that song, how did it go?

Eyes, and ears, and mouth, and nose!

Head, shoulders, knees, and toes! Knees and toes!

Adam had lovely toes, she remembers those. Up until the age of nine, at which point his feet were the same size as hers and not at all adorable.

Now Winnie is contorting her face, trying out its plasticity under the glare. Margot did all of that with Adam too. The face pulling. The pouts. The nostril flares. The monster snarls. Tricks with her spectacles. Small children love that stuff. Margot knew it was important to trust her own instincts, to play with the boy, to respond to his interests, to develop a bond. She'd read Dr. Spock. She'd read Winnicott.

She liked to turn on the record player in the lounge room and dance with him. They would spin around together, and squeal with abandon, and for a few minutes Margot would feel the consuming flow of action. But she loved her child the very most when he was asleep, when she was able to feel contented by the fact of his existence, while having a respite from attending to his needs. She looked forward to Adam growing up, and she enjoyed his company as a boy, when he was well behaved yet funny, funnier than most people she knew.

How did he get so funny? Margot asked John once, delighted.

Oh, come on, John replied. Have you met his mother?

Adam was rather a self-conscious young man—aren't they all?—but still a pleasure to be around, and she accepted him as he got older and replicated his father. She was very fond of his father, of course, so there were worse people their son could have replicated if he was determined to be unoriginal. Then, later, Margot appreciated Adam's choice of mate. Grace, lovely Grace, whose grace extended to her maternity. Margot was so optimistic that Grace and she would be friends. What happened there?

Why did Margot say Grace was a natural in that brief conversation with Hilary Fuller? A natural. What a flippant word. What an imbecilic word. What a loaded word. Did Margot mean fertile? Patient? Maternal? Those qualities that are meant to be inherent to the female of breeding age?

No, I didn't mean any of those things, Margot understands now. I meant that I was disappointed—I am disappointed—by how easily Grace put her own life aside when motherhood happened to her.

Grace's work colleagues made a fuss about her pregnancy. They organized a drinks event (mocktails only) and pooled their funds to give her a hamper on her last day of work before maternity leave. The hamper contained, according to its gift tag, carefully curated items essential for the baby journey: fair-trade herbal teas and bamboo baby wipes, alpaca booties and natural rubber pacifiers, a sheepskin teddy bear and several tiny snap-crotch singlets made from certified organic cotton.

The full hamper was sitting on Adam and Grace's kitchen table when Margot popped over one night on her way home from the university. She wanted to speak to them about John's medical care. She was even considering broaching the unspoken fact of his violence. The night before he'd woken in the dark and repeatedly punched her bicep with one fist and squeezed her forearm with the other hand to anchor himself. The outburst woke her from a deep sleep. She had scrambled away in shock, fled the bedroom and curled up on the couch in the lounge until the sun came up. Perhaps I was snoring, she thought. Perhaps he was having a nightmare, like a child who wakes up flailing and frightened. In the morning, John was a doddery sweetheart and confused that Margot wasn't in their bed. She did not mention the outburst to him. If it hadn't been for the lurid blotches all over her arm, she might have convinced herself it hadn't occurred.

Margot saw the hamper on the kitchen table, and decided not to comment on it. She spotted a fluffy gray hat with bear-shaped ears and realized she had no interest in discovering the rest of the contents. But Grace noticed her noticing.

I wanted to wait until you got here before I unpacked it, she explained to Margot, rubbing her hands together. Gift from everyone at work!

Oh?

Grace finished up at work today, Adam explained.

Did you forget? Grace seemed surprised.

Of course not, Margot said, already irritated. And then she stood beside her daughter-in-law as the hamper was emptied of its contents.

Grace cooed over the objects. Margot pushed up her shirtsleeves and pulled them down again and pretended to be interested.

Boobs and a blanket, Margot announced to the kitchen. A few nappies. That's all you really need with a new baby. And then she went home, without talking to Adam and Grace about anything much at all.

Before the hamper, there'd been the invitation to the baby shower, which Margot declined with a work-related excuse. After the hamper, there was the suggestion that Margot might accompany Grace to a baby superstore to choose a cot. I'd rather stick flaming needles in my eyes, Margot thought about that invitation, also declined.

After Lily was born, Margot was enraptured and affectionate. She took a couple of days off work to help when Adam and Grace brought Lily home from hospital, and she was practical and gentle with both the oozing new mother and Adam, who was stunned by the fact of the infant. But Margot quickly left them to it, without much pining for the newborn.

Just last week, with Lily now a bonny seven-month-old baby, Grace told Margot she didn't intend to return to work when her maternity leave ended, that she was loving being at home with

Lily, and that it was the best and most important thing she'd ever done.

Margot cannot recall her precise response to that announcement, but she knows—she knows now in the dread of her stomach—that it was ungenerous.

Margot stirs in her chair, crosses her arms and legs.

I have not lost my reason, Winnie says on stage, her eyes squinting, her forehead frowning. *Not yet.*

It's unlikely that reason is going to help her now, stuck in the earth and babbling. It seems wholly unreasonable to keep perpetuating reason's glory. I think, therefore I am, eh? What bollocks. Damn this Cartesian performance. Damn this horrible play.

Stay focused, Margot thinks. Keep thinking.

Have I been unkind about Grace's joy? Yes. Yes, I have.

Am I uninterested in their baby? Well, I'm not reaching the expected grandmotherly levels of obsession.

And this is why my son is angry with me. He's always had a supercilious side, of course, but the real disdain, the judgmental remarks about my every move, they started with Grace's pregnancy. I made it too apparent it was no dream of mine to be a grandmother. That is a taboo position even more problematic than motherly ambivalence.

Oh, Margot, you fool, how did you not realize this already? It's one thing to hold views on maternity that might not be universally palatable, but it's quite another thing to inflict them on your own son and daughter-in-law. What a failure of the imagination it is, to dismiss Grace's way of being as unenlightened or retrograde or dull. What a narrow old bitch you've been.

Hang on a minute. She could have been worse. Margot thinks of Jan, one of her colleagues who opted not to have children—a woman, obviously, as the choice was largely incidental to men of their generation. Jan is disdainful toward any academic who gets pregnant. According to her, a pregnancy bump is the announcement of a distinct lack of professional and intellectual ambition. She's not serious about her research, is she? Jan will say. Not if she wants a baby. How did you let that happen? Jan once asked a PhD student, glaring at her pregnant body, like she'd forgotten the basics of human reproduction.

We all started with our mothers, Jan. Even you.

Yes, Margot could have been worse. She wasn't as bad as Jan. But still.

The bell. It hurts like a knife. A gouge . . .

How often I have said, Ignore it, Winnie . . . pay no heed.

On stage, Winnie is blaming herself for the torture being inflicted on her by the wretched buzzing bell. She is trying to use her remaining reason to convince herself that it is possible to be unbothered by a harsh too-loud buzz that only sounds when one is almost asleep.

Good grief, Winnie, is there no end to our potential for self-flagellation?

Perhaps I need to be more self-flagellating with Grace and Adam, Margot thinks. I could try to be honest about my feelings toward being a mother and a grandmother, and I could apologize for being insensitive to them. Yes. I could do that. And then, well, then maybe I could talk to them about the other thing. About John.

When I leave the theater tonight, I will get onto it, Margot thinks, sitting up in her seat. I will send Adam a text message as soon as I get to the car. I will say I need to visit them in the next couple of days. And he will reply immediately because it's late and he will suspect there's a problem.

Well, good. There is a problem. And he might ask me why I need to visit, and I will say that I want to talk to them. I will be firm. He might even dial my number after I've piqued his curiosity. What's the matter, Mum? he might ask. That exasperated tone of his.

The thought of Adam dialing her number tonight makes Margot suddenly hot. Of course, there might not be any mobile coverage in the car park. That's always a variable.

But she will try. She knows she must be in touch with him before she changes her mind. She must stay emboldened before she disappears again inside the rush of her life. She must.

Adam will be surprised by any apology from Margot about Lily and Grace, or any revelation about John. Adam will struggle to comprehend the current situation between his parents. He's their child with a child's blind spot about his parents' complexities. And they've barely even fought in front of him.

There is my story of course, when all else fails.

Winnie has now turned to praising the power of narrative. Well, that's a move forward from reason.

Tell your story. But which one? We need to choose our story, and recognize it, in order to tell it to anyone else.

And then how to tell it? When to tell it?

There was such volatility between Margot and John in the early days. Adam would be surprised to learn about that.

Margot remembers one fight on a grassy nature strip only a few months after they began dating. They were crossing the road together, bickering. Before they made it to the other side, they were yelling. Margot stopped on the nature strip and stormed off along the cushiony green ground, traffic zooming past her in both directions. John jogged to her, grabbed her arm, and she spun around. They stood facing each other, possibly weeping, definitely shouting. After a few minutes of that, Margot stormed off again and walked a decent distance before she looked around to see that John had stayed in place, bent over, his palms resting on his thighs, head dropped down as though he were puffed, as though he had just finished running a race. Margot flopped onto the grass and sat, cross-armed and cross-ankled (wearing her brown mini), on the nature strip until John ambled up beside her and sat down too. It was the afternoon. They hadn't been drinking. People filled both footpaths—the one they'd left and the one they hadn't reached—and Margot and John had made what could only be described as a scene. Margot snapped out of the fight and realized she'd lost control in public, and that John too had lost control in public. She was twenty-three years old, mortified that she was the type of person to have a public screaming match.

But somewhere else, deeper than the embarrassment, she also sensed a tingling thrill. To feel so much and share such passion and to be—even for a few moments—the center of a real drama. This was a real love affair, she thought. This was the real thing.

Margot and John soon stopped performing their passion, unless privately, and developed a sense of public decorum. They learned to understand enough about each other so that they could choose whether to antagonize the other person, rather than it happening unintentionally through exasperated confusion. They were harmonious. People envied them their marital longevity. And Margot never again had cause to question the type of person she had become within their relationship.

Until the recent violence.

Until tonight.

Until she considered what Ivy Parker would think of the esteemed professor being hurt by her husband. Until she imagined telling her son about it at last.

So, is Margot the type of person to have public screaming matches? Yes. Is Margot the type of person to be bruised by her husband? Yes.

But what misguided questions.

Margot suspects that there is no such thing as a type of person who is more susceptible to a particular behavior. There are only situations, and we do not know what will become of us until we are inside each new one.

Eight

Summer has missed the first few minutes of the second act, only now sitting down off the aisle at the back of the auditorium. She adjusts herself in her seat, smiles briefly at the man in the wheelchair beside her, and looks to the stage. Oh, Winnie.

Summer slides her hand inside her right trouser pocket and grips her phone so she will feel any vibration. If April gets in touch. If that guy Joel gets in touch. If Summer feels any quiver from her phone at all, she will stand up straightaway and professionally exit the space.

Joel was easy to find in the crowd at the end of intermission with his ginger hair and April's king parrot squawking from his arm skin. Summer took him to the staffroom, told him the news about the fires and the wind change, tried to explain about her girlfriend, April, and Woolf the dog, and April's parents, and his parents, and where they all were and what they were doing, as far as she could ascertain from the cut-off conversations she'd just had with April.

It took him a while to respond to her barrage of information.

You're April's girl? Amazing. I had the biggest crush on her as a kid. For years.

Summer let Joel use her phone charger to get out of the red. As soon as his mobile's battery came back to life, several missed messages buzzed at him.

Oh shit, he said, sitting down on the seat in the locker room.

Summer nodded and touched his arm. It's not a good situation, she said.

He covered his face with his hands for a moment and rubbed his palms vigorously across his cheeks as though to bring the blood there, as though the blood might carry forward an answer or a clarity. Then he sniffed and shook his head in an attempt to adjust to a new equilibrium.

As the danger dawned on Joel, Summer made sure to maintain a demeanor of calm competence. She didn't want to be like the person crying at the funeral who the rest of the people at the funeral have never seen, so that the rest of the people all wonder, Who does that person think she is? Why does that person think this grief is hers to howl? Don't make this all about you, Sum.

Joel's family home is in peril. His parents are in peril. April is in a car a fair distance from the fires. April will be fine.

April will be fine.

They walked back up to the foyer together. Summer gave Joel her number and asked him to keep her in the loop.

He said he didn't know what he was going to do but thought he'd probably try to find his sisters. He said he'd been loving the play.

I was super keen to see what was going to happen to that poor lady, Joel said as he waved goodbye to Summer and headed back into the hot night.

He was a nice enough guy, and he'd crushed on April as a kid, so that's endearing.

On stage, Winnie is now only a head in a mound. That's what's happened to the poor lady, Joel. Her dire predicament has become infinitely worse.

Winnie is remembering a doll.

A little white straw hat with a chin elastic . . . China blue eyes that open and shut.

Winnie's own eyes open and shut mechanically against the light on her.

Blink.

Blink.

Blink.

Winnie's own hat is a little black feathery hat, perhaps held in place with a long hatpin, but not a chin elastic. Beneath her hat, her hair also remains. It is unruly and thinly spun like fairy floss, no longer contained in any way that could be described as a do.

Winnie's mound is a pile of garbage now. That's what's going on in this second act, Summer is sure of it. That is what we are meant to perceive.

Summer is watching a pile of garbage with a woman's head at the top of the pile. Winnie's head, like a plastic doll's, pulled off its cloth body and dropped onto the ground. It just so happens that this detached head landed neck down in the earth, hat on, hair up, face forward facing the sun.

The grass on the mound appears drier in this act. Sparser.

The color of the mound and the color of Winnie's stunned face are both a muted noncolor that merge together, indistinguishable and deathly.

The contents of Winnie's bag are strewn all over the mound.

The contents of Winnie's bag, so organized earlier, look like litter now, like plastic objects found in a waterway and laid out to be photographed for consciousness-raising purposes, Winnie's head just one of the things that might be collected and bagged for more appropriate disposal.

Appropriate disposal. Now there's a concept for our times.

Summer remembers when she first learned about waste disposal as a child, the curious fact of where the contents of the rubbish bins go. She was eight years old and felt embarrassed that she hadn't before thought about it properly, even with a mother who always put the food scraps in a fetid ice-cream container on the kitchen bench. Summer knew how to stake a tomato seedling by the age of four, and when the compost was ready for the veggie patch. She knew to use both sides of her drawing paper and what types of packaging could be recycled. But the actual garbage, the smelly stuff inside the swing bin in her house or the rubbish bins on the streets, she had not previously understood its final destination.

It's called landfill, her friend explained to her. The garbage trucks empty their collections into a giant hole in the ground. And it stinks.

Wow, said Summer.

And then, once the giant hole's all filled up, entire worlds are built on top of the rubbish, and you'd never even know it was there.

Summer took some time to process this new and miraculous information.

Maybe in hundreds of years, archaeologists (she knew about archaeologists) will dig up our towns, she said, and our broken rubbish will be examined and treasured like ancient Egyptian artifacts.

These days, Summer knows a great deal more about waste management. More than necessary. Far more than necessary. She knows how waste—all kinds—is shipped around the globe on massive barges from places unable, unwilling, to manage disposal to places that are apparently better able to manage disposal. She knows that tons of garbage are burned in giant bonfires visible from space and that the toxic air pollution spawned is better than the rubbish only because the smoke particles are softer and more dispersed than the rubbish particles. She knows that no matter how diligently people sort their glass from their cardboards from their plastics, it hardly makes a difference because much of it is unlikely to get treated separately. She knows that China recently decided to close their recycling industry and leave the world's waste in limbo, unable to be dealt with where it was generated, unable to be dragged across the earth and dumped on another landmass. The very idea that rubbish is shipped around the world for disposal—the sheer impractical extremity of that—makes Summer feel physically sick, and, even then, after going to those insane measures, the problem is not solved. It is probably unsolvable.

She saw a Facebook clip of an economist decrying the microconsumer attempts to fix waste accumulation in the oceans. Banning plastic straws was his example. All that energy and guilt wasted on campaigns to stop people from sticking a tube of plastic in their milkshakes when the bulk of ocean waste—the heavy clogging tons of it—is composed of discarded fishing nets.

Oh, the ocean waste. Gyres. Vortexes. Islands. There are islands of waste—one of which, Summer understands, is twice the size of France—swirling insistently in the Pacific waters. A garbage mass twice the size of a significant country. She cannot understand it. She cannot.

Summer has dreams about rubbish. She dreams about white plastic bags piling up under her bed, their moist noxious contents bubbling visibly inside. Often it is bags of meat in her dreams, offcuts or offal or both, tumbling red and half-pulverized out of their soft containers and onto the dusty floorboards. Summer wakes up during the night, smelling the waste, smelling the discarded meat, and swings her head down, throws her hand beneath her body to check for the piles of bags. Even when the bags aren't there—and they are never there—Summer needs to concentrate on convincing herself that she cannot smell something rancid.

Last week, she woke from a rubbish dream, noted the lack of bags, kept sniffing, sniffing, sure that there was blood in the air. It was a hot night, her naked body was covered in sweat, and it took her a fretful hour to realize that the moisture between her legs wasn't perspiration, that she'd forgotten her period was due, and that there was some blood on the fitted sheet.

You can't smell it, April said wearily. Fresh blood doesn't smell. Go back to sleep, Sum.

The rubbish dreams have become more frequent since this theater season started, since Summer saw this play with this woman in this prison of waste.

It isn't good for me, she thinks. It's triggering.

Summer wishes that she were more even-tempered. She wishes she noticed less and worried less and cared less. She knows there are better ways to live a functional life. Well, she hopes that there might be better ways to live a functional life and she just hasn't worked them out yet.

She knows she shouldn't blame Winnie and the play for her nightmares and her looping thoughts and her fucking pooling sweat and shortened breaths and enormous yearnings to cry in public places. Almost everything she encounters feels triggering.

Summer's mum occasionally asks her how her anxiety is going. The question arrives in a text message or over the phone. It never comes when they're together in person, when Summer has a break from work and uni and flies back to WA. Summer has the impression that her mum fits in asking the question—How's your anxiety going, Sum?—like she fits in writing a shopping list or making an appointment or googling a person she's been meaning to find out a little bit more about. So Summer never answers her properly. Summer gives a casual answer to the casual question.

The usual.

Not too bad.

Fine.

Thanks for asking.

And Summer's mother leaves it there. Or sends a love emoji.

On stage now, Winnie is seeking to understand the limits of her reality—what she experiences from the outside world, and what emerges from within.

I do of course hear cries. But they are in my head surely.

Summer squeezes her phone. It shudders.

She pulls it from her pocket. Nothing. No messages. She must have made it shudder herself. Okay.

She slides it back inside her trousers. She tries to loosen the grip of her fingers around the device but they are holding hard.

April will be fine.

April will be fine.

April will be fine.

Maybe I'm protecting Mum, Summer thinks. With my nonanswers to her question. Is there another way I could talk to her about what's going on in my head? Could I attempt uncensored honesty? What would that sound like?

How's your anxiety going, Sum?

Thanks for asking, Mum. Last week I walked down Bourke Street with April. We were going to visit some bookstores on our way to see a band in a beer garden—peak Melbourne day, should have been a dream. But then we passed the old café with the iconic neon sign where the lovely owner was killed in the middle of the day by some crazy terrorist with a gun. And it was the first time I've been past the café since that happened and it gave me waves of dread just stepping on the same footpath where his body had been. I was positive I could see bloodstains on the concrete. And I hated all the new bollards that have been installed along the busiest thoroughfares to make it more difficult for drivers to drive their cars into pedestrians. I hated the bollards, even the ones that have been yarn bombed. Maybe especially the ones that have been yarn bombed. And I didn't want to be on those city streets at all. I wanted to be home under the covers, clinging to my love, watching a TV program that never ends.

But you can't let them win, Summer! her mum might say then. That's what the terrorists want—for everyone to live in fear!

Yes, we must go about our days. We must enjoy ourselves. I've heard the platitudes. I know we are all meant to be defiantly oblivious, but maybe I could avoid all unsafe places? I am very scared of dying.

Where are the unsafe places, Sum?

There are no safe places, Mum.

Darling, you need to have a more positive attitude!

There were neo-Nazis on the beach over the summer, spitting their hate onto the sand. And swastikas sprayed on nursing home walls. And police officers displaying white pride. And hate speeches in parliament. And mass shootings inside churches and mosques and schools and concert halls and malls. And women murdered in their homes. And people brutalized in cells.

So, obviously not war zones, borders, prisons, and refugee camps, but also not beaches, schools, nursing homes, private homes, places of worship, police stations, shopping centers, government buildings, concert halls, or city streets could accurately be described as safe places.

Do you feel unsafe at concerts, Sum? You love concerts!

Mum, my last big concert was Taylor Swift. April knew how much I loved Tay Tay when I was little, so she surprised me with the tickets. It was not the sort of thing we'd normally go to but April thinks Taylor is sweetly hot and possibly closeted, so there were enough reasons for her to find the idea interesting. I started feeling waves of panic as soon as we exited the train station near the stadium. The area was like a bunker—all partitions and concrete barriers—and it felt too contained. It felt nothing like going to a festival, where there are tall trees dotted in the distance and people gathering wherever, and you can stay on the edges if you choose. Outside the train station, there were crowds of people, and the people were mainly young and happy, and then the Manchester bombing dropped into my mind and would not leave.

Remember, Mum? When a man bombed an Ariana Grande concert in the UK because the place was teeming with nubile and joyful girls who needed to be destroyed? That concert was promoting an album called *Dangerous Woman*. Some of the victims were wearing *Dangerous Woman* T-shirts. You cannot make this stuff up. And so I started to panic hard about how that little girl with the kitten ears might look if she were shot. Or that beautiful pair of boys wearing matching faux-snakeskin leggings. Or the group of teenagers in their schoolgirl sexy minis. And how far a bomb's explosion could reach. If it went off in this block of seats, would it get all the way to that block of seats where the middle-aged mother is dancing with her eight-year-old, both of them covered in glitter and flowers? And how would those red stiletto boots on that girl over there manage in a crowd crush? All I could see were potential victims. It was morbid and it was heavy but those were the thoughts inside my head and the only way I got through the concert was by popping a beta-blocker during the support act and guzzling a serious quantity of potent peach daiquiris. And I sang.

I shouted and danced and screamed and sang, and clung to April like a limpet.

Summer adjusts her body in her chair. She tries to ground herself in the space she is in right now. She needs to stop thinking about what she would say if she were to answer her mother truthfully. It is obviously impossible to answer her mother truthfully.

Summer needs to watch the play.

To sing too soon is fatal, I always find, Winnie says. *On the other hand it is possible to leave it too late.*

What the fuck?

These words. This play. Why is Winnie pondering the power of song?

Breathe, Summer. Breathe.

She counts in for four, holds her breath for three, counts out for eight. Counts in for four, holds her breath for three, counts out for eight.

April is fine.

Counts in for four, holds her breath for three, counts out for eight.

April is fine.

Summer is sitting in the theater.

Her feet are on the floor inside her black Docs, inside her white socks. Her feet are pressed to the floor. She is still. She is grounded. Summer is watching the play.

One cannot sing . . . It bubbles up, for some unknown reason . . . one chokes it back.

Winnie, please talk about something else, something other than singing. Singing is good. I sang through my panic at Tay Tay, and it bubbled up inside the bubbles and the lasers and the beaming rainbows, and it was good.

Singing was the release of the choke, not the choke itself.

Counts in for four, holds her breath for three, counts out for eight.

April is fine.

Counts in for four, holds her breath for three, counts out for eight.

Summer feels inside her trouser pockets.

On the right side, there is her phone, still and silent and unhelpful.

On the left side, there are three sticks from ice creams and a drinks receipt. Summer fingers the sticks and the piece of paper inside the polyester lining of her pocket. She thinks about the ice cream that covered the sticks and the hungry licks from other people's tongues that cleaned the little pieces of wood so that now they could be mistaken for craft materials, ready to be made into something wonky and educational.

One of the ice-cream sticks is not completely smooth. A tiny lump remains on the otherwise stripped object. Summer picks at the lump with her fingernail until it releases. She takes her hand out and cleans the crumb of chocolate from under her nail with her teeth.

I've just eaten the dregs of someone's intermission snack, she thinks. That is probably all kinds of wrong. But that intermission was all kinds of wrong already. Trying to talk to April, the fires, the fucking phone, Joel, Professor Pierce being a bit of a cow about her lecture.

And what was with the pretty woman at the end, when the intermission bell was chiming, asking me about the Indigenous art in the function room?

Does the audience think the ushers get educated about the painting collections? Don't they understand that we're trained in how to use a ticket-scanning gun and how to be accommodating—within reason—to the general public, and how to stealthily open and close doors, but that we are not given a cultural education about what's on the walls just in case someone, once or twice a year, is curious? The cultural training provided to the ushers comes with the opportunity, as they say, to watch world-class theater and to rub up against people of influence when those people of influence are having trouble reading their seat number and might need a younger pair of eyes to decipher the printout.

Every now and then, a member of the audience will sidle up to Summer, during intermission or once the show is over, and attempt to have a chat. Summer has on several occasions been asked out for a nightcap by some sleaze feigning fascination in her theatrical opinions. Once, she made the mistake of attempting to fob off a man by saying she had to get up early the following day to go to uni.

Let me guess what you're studying, the man said, buttoning his suit jacket over his large gut as he performed his contemplation of her. Let me have a good, long think about this.

Drama, Summer said, trying to cut short the interaction. I'm an acting student.

Ha! the man said. Even better. So let's talk! About. Drama. Over a cocktail or two.

As I said, Summer insisted, I've got to get up early and would prefer to go straight home.

Little bitch, he said, before storming off toward the car park.

The lady who asked about the paintings wasn't hitting on her—that was clear—even though Summer immediately registered that she was attractive and dressed how she'd like to think she might dress when she is a bit older, cooler, and properly financed. No, that wasn't it. And she was sort of nice about working in hospo, and those terrible trays.

The lady had asked the staff in the function room about the art, but then she walked up to Summer, went out of her way to ask Summer, even though Summer was in a different section of the foyer as the intermission ended, diddling around with ice-cream sticks and trying not to freak out entirely about April's situation.

I suppose she asked me about the pictures because she thought I was Aboriginal, like the artist, and I might know about the art or take an interest in it because of that. As though life works like that, Summer thinks. She probably imagined me sitting on red desert sands in a circle of women, illustrating our totems. Some wholesome and idyllic stereotype. Oh, I wish. I fucking wish.

If random white women are going to make assumptions about my heritage, Summer thinks, I really need to cut down Mum's commitment to color blindness as an exalted personal virtue.

It doesn't matter what color we are, she's often said, like a children's TV presenter. It's what's inside that counts.

What a crock. Maybe Summer's mother needs to know how often her own daughter is alerted to her non-whiteness when she's minding her own business doing her job going about her day trying to live her life.

When Summer started primary school, her teacher separated the class into cultural groupings, a very dubious pedagogy now that Summer remembers it. Summer was put with the black kids. She didn't question her teacher that day. She went along with the games they were told to play and she mentioned it to her mum when she got home among the list of the things they'd done at school—there was guided reading, there was counting in tens, there was lunch eating, there was the part where we got to talk about being Aboriginal. But then, a couple of days later, Summer was moved into the other, bigger, paler group of children when it was time for Cultural Inquiry.

Cultural Inquiry. That's what it was called, and isn't that a pithy summary for everything that hasn't gone on between Summer and her mother ever since, even when Summer was cast as an Aboriginal girl in a play as a teenager—You certainly look the part, her drama teacher declared.

Summer thought that play might have been a chance to ask her mother about the identity that hovered around her. She thought the story of the girl in the play whose own heritage is suppressed might have been the trigger for a truth. But no, even then, just another non-conversation. After Summer's final performance, her mum gave her a bunch of banksias and praised her for remembering so many lines.

Summer knows she needs to speak to her mother about her father. She needs to get past the layers of defensiveness that have smothered them all her life. She needs to not let her mother make another joke or resort to a platitude when Summer attempts to bring up her father.

Summer is ashamed to realize that it's been a couple of years since she last tried to get to the truth of it, during a boozy Christmas lunch when one of her cousins (on the Scottish side) made a racist remark about Australian history.

Summer corrected her cousin, reminding him that the country didn't start with Captain fucking Cook.

What are you? he said to her. An angry Abo?

Summer jolted against the dining table like she'd been shoved in the chest.

Shut up, she said to her cousin. You're an idiot.

He made an inane woo-hoooo noise as though it was a low-level turn-on to see Summer so annoyed.

Here is what Summer needs to say to her mother. You're a freckly white woman, Mum. I am not. Just tell me who you slept with.

That could be my opening grenade, Summer thinks. Straight in there.

Just tell me who my father is.

Perhaps Summer could provide her with options, like a multiple-choice questionnaire, to make the process easier.

Was he an activist you met one afternoon when you were being a good ally at a demo? Did you go to the pub afterward and flirt with the charismatic, aggressive demo leader? Were you flattered he found your pasty limbs attractive even for that one night? That he forgave you for being a First Fleeter?

Was he just a nice boy you knew from school who seduced you on the beach one night, both of you drunk and careless?

Was he a stranger you hooked up with who didn't mean anything to you?

Was he someone else's man?

Was he a writer you fangirled at a festival, and you were the person he shagged in WA before he returned to his uni job in Sydney?

Was he a muso or a footy player at a bar, confident and horny after a solid performance?

Was he dignified and beautiful, but committed elsewhere?

Or just a womanizing arsehole?

Was he even Indigenous? Or is everyone barking up the wrong tree?

I know he didn't rape you, but that is a depressing singular detail to know about one's father. I want to know the rest. You are not protecting me by keeping me ignorant, if that is what you are trying to do, and I am tired of trying to understand what you are trying to do.

I understand that he may not have known about me, or that he might have rejected you, or that you might have rejected him. I understand that you raised me alone. I understand that you are a superhero hardworking single mother, but I wish you would stop deflecting my questions and taking offense when I ask them.

It is not an insult to you if I want to know about my father. I am not betraying the sisterhood or undermining motherhood to want to know about my father. I have been telling you forever that you are my favorite person, you are my wonderful mum, you are a great mum, you are the best mum.

Even if my father is a terrible person in some way, or dead, or just irrelevant in your opinion, this is not only about him. He must have relatives, Mum. They would also be mine, and I want them. I want those people. I do not want to wait until you are dead before I know this part of me.

If you think you're protecting me, you do not understand what my life is like already. Don't you remember people asking about me when I was little? Don't you remember the way I was seen? Nothing's changed.

I'm a bit of a mess sometimes, Mum, and maybe, maybe if I got this sorted out, it would help me live better, it would help me be better in the world, somehow.

Yes, that could be a speech.

That could do it.

Summer takes a deep breath and adjusts herself in her chair. She moves her fingers around the ice-cream sticks inside one pocket and her phone inside the other. The phone is surprisingly cold.

What are those exquisite lines?

I wish I could write that speech, Summer thinks. I wish I could write myself a script to rehearse before I speak to Mum.

Maybe I can.

Maybe tomorrow—if tomorrow comes—I will write that script and rehearse it, until the words in my head, the words on the page, don't get stuck in my gullet or stay choked in my body before they become sounds in the world.

Bzzzzzzzz! The bell rings on stage—the harsh, shattering alarm to ensure we all remain awake.

Winnie's face jolts pale inside the rubbish pile as her eyes snap open.

Summer tries to open her own eyes wider.

Watch the play.

April is okay. You will talk to your mum. Watch the play.

Winnie is awake. She is speaking again about the two people who walked past her long ago. *Standing there gaping at me.*

She was stuck in her mound with her torso out, back then. Her ball-gown bodice. Teal silk. Tailored to emphasize the hourglass.

Can't have been a bad bosom.

Seen worse shoulders.

Winnie was propped up for appraisal and could not turn away from it.

Is there any life in her legs?

That's the key question, Summer thinks. Are the buried parts of her body the dead parts of her? Is the hill of rubbish that is consuming her body just a concrete metaphor for the death that is rising over her?

Maybe this woman is not a living person, trapped. Maybe she's a dead person, expiring incrementally. Is there a difference?

Summer has not thought about Winnie's burial being about the burial of a dead body. Fuck. Maybe this is zombie theater.

This morning an ad appeared on Summer's Insta feed that she couldn't scroll past in the way she dismissed the other ads for the other products that some algorithm decided she might desire. This ad was not for period underpants or ethical footwear or alternative banking institutions. This ad was for eco-egg burials. On point, thought Summer. Well done, algorithm.

Summer clicked it. A pair of cool European industrial designers had noticed the amount of waste generated after a cool European industrial design show, and they got thinking not only about the waste created by human beings, but the waste of human beings themselves. The designers wanted to do something about the problems of burying dead humans—the space it demands, the pollution it generates—so they created eggs for people to be buried inside. Small ones for human cremains, large ones for curled-up corpses, handmade from biodegradable starch that would allow the ashes or the body to seep into the surrounding earth and provide nutrients for plant growth. The eco-eggs in the images were all topped with a spindly seedling covered in promising buds of green.

The product made no sense to Summer. The eco-eggs solved a problem only if there was some elusive expanse of land that could not be used as a graveyard but could be used for reforestation. She was weirded out by the rebirthing aspect of the eggs, and their extraordinary cost. The price did not include the plant. Customers were advised to source their own seedlings from a local nursery to be ready for planting once the eco-egg arrived from Italy.

After making the mistake of clicking the ad and reading every page on the eco-egg site, Summer then got herself buried in an internet wormhole about eco-death alternatives. A booming market.

The corpse as consumer. The consuming corpse. Consuming the corpse.

It's not enough to be paranoid about how to live an ethical life, we must also be ethical in death. You can get wrapped in linen and planted in a bush block for composting purposes, or cryofrozen before your bodily cells are shattered and scattered into a scientific ether. Or you can go full benevolent, donating your corpse to be chopped up for educative purposes by blundering living people who need to see all the human body parts for real. Summer despises the thought of an undergraduate medical student scraping through her internal yellow fat, but she could probably adjust that point of view as she gets older. If she gets older.

There's not always a body to fuss over after death. Certain modes of dying can do the disposal and the dispersal of the cells at once. There wouldn't be much left of a human body killed in a bushfire, if the human body was really in the heat of it, at the hot core of the flames. Death as cremation.

Where is April?

Where is Summer's most beloved human being right now? Where is that body in this moment?

A throbbing starts in Summer's ears.

She thinks of April's body—her tattoos exposed and concealed.

She thinks of her organs, her fat, her muscles, her hair, her nails, her strong beautiful legs, colorful and bare in summer shorts. She'd be wearing shorts right now. And some flimsy tank top.

Summer pictures the pictures on April's flesh, and she pictures them burning, smoking, melting, cooking, like pork crackling in an oven. Fuck. Not April. Not April.

Unhook from that thought, Summer.

Burning heart on her chest.

Bubbling hot-air balloons on her left leg.

Melting Matilda on her right.

External ovary next to her hipbone. Oh, those hipbones. Fuck.

Crackling fallopian tubes across her belly.

Let go of those images.

Watch them go.

Watch them go.

Oh god. No. What's wrong with my brain? How can I even come up with these thoughts? My April.

Breathe, Summer. Breathe.

She counts in for four, holds her breath for three, counts out for eight. Counts in for four, holds her breath for three, counts out for eight.

April is fine.

Counts in for four, holds her breath for three, counts out for eight.

April is fine.

Summer is sitting in the theater.

I am sitting in the theater, she thinks. I am here.

April is fine.

April will be fine.

And soon this will be over and I will contact her again. I'm not going to stand on the stairs like I'm meant to during the applause, nodding and smiling at all the people as they exit the theater. I will run to the staffroom as soon as the play finishes and I will get out of here as fast as I can.

I will find April. I will hold April. I will.

And I can just say I was sick, violently sick. I don't care if I get sacked.

On stage, Winnie suddenly screams.

Winnie's scream is a new sound but it is also the first sound, the oldest sound, the truest sound. She screams and screams.

Inside the polyester of her trouser pocket, Summer's phone pulses against her fingers.

Nine

Winnie stops screaming.

Ivy shifts in her chair and shares with Hilary a fast, wide-eyed glance in the dark of the theater.

That was a horrifying scream, their wide eyes say to each other. That was uncomfortable to hear.

Ivy again admires Hilary's profile watching the play, just as she did during the first act, noting her new hairstyle visible in the light from the stage. Ivy forgot to mention at intermission how much she likes Hilary's hair. She is annoyed with herself for that. Ivy wants to be someone who says the compliment, not someone who thinks the compliment but does not say it.

There have been times in Ivy's life when a single warm sentence from another person has made the difference between wanting to die and not wanting to die that day. After Rupert, if a guy in a shop so much as handled her purchases with care or asked about her afternoon, Ivy would absorb a rush of replenishing tenderness. It wouldn't last long, but there it was, keeping her going for another moment.

Ivy knows what a glint of kindness can do for another person, so she tries to be careful with her interactions, feeling for potential impact, choosing her words. Ivy can still be fierce or direct or rude to people, but rarely by accident.

Hilary is a mostly contented person—even-tempered, even—and Ivy complimenting her hair would likely make no difference to her overall mood. Still, Ivy can't help weighing down such a simple thing with all these connotations. She cannot un-know what she knows about the precariousness of the human soul.

Winnie is speaking again.

The sounds produced inside her mouth are forming words again now.

The words are preferable to the screams despite the words becoming more and more of a frazzled ramble.

It is probable that Winnie's head is hurting her, that the effort of continuing to speak without a body to push the sound out is generating considerable pain. And yet, she continues. . . . *What on earth could possibly be the matter . . .*

Oh, let's see, Winnie, Ivy thinks.

What on earth could be wrong?

What could be wrong on earth?

What possibility is there on earth?

What matter is possible?

What on earth in earth of earth could be wrong?

No. Can't think, Winnie. Can't think of an answer at all.

The second act of this play is different to Ivy's memories of it from the other performances she's seen. In Roussillon, in Bristol, there wasn't the explicit deterioration of the landscape that has happened here.

There was the sinking of the woman into the earth. There was that.

There was the ground strangling the woman around her neck. There was her entrapment and her head poking out, chattering on. There was that.

But the earth didn't die so blatantly during intermission, as it has now, tonight, in this production.

In Bristol and Roussillon, there was just the same mound of dry grass—same size, same color, same angle and position on the stage—for the duration of the performance. But this hill here, in this second act, is bleaker, with Winnie's belongings strewn all over it like a postapocalyptic wasteland and her poor head the last living thing on the well-dead earth. An animate face with a bird corpse perched on top of it, shoved through the surface of a disaster-scape.

During intermission, Ivy talked to the general manager of the company about the director of this production.

She's an ecofeminist activist, he explained to Ivy. So her

vision of Beckett is imbued with that sensibility. You can see it in her choices.

The staging of this second act must be what the GM was talking about.

The mess of belongings strewn across the stage. The destroyed and depleted earth. Those details are not in the script, Ivy is sure of it. Dying earth, definitely, but not dead earth. That distinction is everything. That distinction is where the hope hides.

I'm an ecofeminist activist too, Ivy wanted to say to the general manager. I care about the environment and its inhabitants. Isn't any thinking person an ecofeminist nowadays? Isn't ecofeminist simply synonymous with enlightened, or kind, or justice-seeking?

How pleasing it would be to publicly define yourself in that way, with such pretend precision. Ivy might add ecofeminist to her biography on the Parker Foundation website.

Ivy Parker, Ecofeminist Philanthropist. That sounds good.

Ivy didn't express those thoughts to the GM. Instead, she spoke to him about their shared vision for the directors' program. Ivy confirmed she was going to grant the required funds. She reiterated her commitment to making theater more accessible for practitioners, as well as for the audience. She hinted at other possibilities around subsidized ticketing.

The general manager was delighted. He gave Ivy a peck on the cheek then tapped his champagne flute against hers.

Now I want you to meet the Glasses, he said. Wonderful people. They're funding a queer workshop series.

The GM pulled Ivy toward the baby boomer couple who had the seats next to her in the theater. The snoring man. The silent woman.

Daniel and Miriam Glass! he shouted, whacking Daniel on the upper arm in a brotherly greeting. The Glass siblings!

The introductions were made.

The Glass siblings? Ivy smiled. So they are brother and sister, not husband and wife, as she'd assumed.

Yes, said Daniel. We sound like a vaudeville act, don't we? The Glass Siblings are simply smashing! Tadaaa!

The man whose face was a waxy mask when he slept during the play was transformed into a demonstrative, cute person. It was remarkable.

Our spouses died within a year of each other, Miriam told Ivy as the men began a separate conversation. Soon after, we settled into our partnership, started our philanthropy. We're a terrific team. We got along so well as children and we get along so well now as old folks. There were just a few decades in there when our loyalties were redirected. But, to be perfectly honest, Danny's been my favorite person my whole life. Is that a terrible thing to admit?

Not at all, Ivy said. You're lucky to have each other.

That's what I think, Miriam nodded, her helmet-y bob tilting back and forth. That's what I think.

Does he always snore at the theater? Ivy asked.

Without fail.

He doesn't want to watch the performance?

It's astounding how much he takes in, even when seemingly unconscious.

A waiter broke their circle then and presented a tray of hors d'oeuvres—a pile of Dutch carrots doused in honey sauce. The snipped green tops were the handle to hold while nibbling.

Haven't seen a carrot on a tray for years, Miriam said, plucking one off the pile.

My grandson told me that if we didn't have nerves in our fingers, we could snap off the ends of our own pinkies as easily as a carrot tip, Daniel announced.

I hope not, said Ivy.

My nieces are going to love that, the GM said. Can't wait to tell them.

I looked it up online, Daniel continued. The thought made me feel sick to the stomach, but I wanted to check if it were true.

And?

It's not, he said. Not at all.

Party pooper, Ivy laughed.

I didn't correct my grandson, said Daniel.

That's the most important thing, Ivy said. Keeping the illusion alive for the children.

Indeed, said Daniel, biting into the carrot he was holding in his fingers and masticating enthusiastically.

It is discomforting to realize how she misjudged the Glasses and made boring assumptions about their relationship and their selves.

Daniel's upper arm in his white shirtsleeve is pressed against Ivy's now. He is asleep, unquietly, and she feels a jolt of embarrassment thinking about how she elbowed him in the first act of the play, and had planned to kick him in the shin, if necessary.

She still cannot stand the sound he is making. She still wouldn't mind shaking him awake and off her, but she will not.

She lets him lean into her. She lets him snore.

She feels a kind of love for this stranger sleeping beside her in the dark.

This is what's so special about theater, Ivy thinks. This forced intimacy between strangers. This shared experience of watching or not watching other people performing right now in this delicate moment. Anything could happen beside me or in front of me, but here I am, sitting here, just doing this play.

My neck is hurting me, Winnie says.

Ivy rotates her head on her vertebrae, aware of the weight of it on her spine. She is grateful for the freedom. She enjoys the small rotations.

But Ivy stops circling her neck, remembering the people sitting behind her. She does not want to bother the people sitting behind her.

Something must move, in the world, I can't any more, Winnie says.

Ivy is relaxing into the second act of the play. She felt quite tense after intermission and her body is finally relaxing, if not her mind.

There was something off with the young usher in the foyer. We were friendly and fine initially, Ivy thinks, but she did not like my question about the art. She called me madam.

Ivy despises being called madam. When did she get old enough to be inflicted with that fawning descriptor? How is it possible she is even close to being old enough for that to be a neutral term to use to address her, in this day and age? She wanted to snap at the young usher.

I don't work in a brothel, she could have said. And I'm not that much older than you. Really, I'm not. Well, I am a couple of decades older than you, but please understand that I do not, will not, cannot think of myself as middle-aged. And I had a baby recently! That's proof, isn't it, proof of my yoof? Just please don't call me madam. I don't want to be your mother. I want to be your friend. Are they my only options? Yes. No. Of course not.

When Hilary and Ivy went to their recent high school reunion, Ivy was horrified by the middle-agedness of her former classmates. There was a woman who had been intimidatingly hip at school, and Ivy only recognized her because of the name tag she had on her chest. Her face had fallen into hound-like dewlaps and there were sun splotches and creases all over her décolletage. She had lank boring hair and was (unironically) dressed in an unflattering long-sleeved blouse with bad jeans. Very bad jeans. And there was an inflection in her voice that was almost satirically pompous. Ivy felt angry with her for aging so badly. Did you have to become so daggy? she wanted to say. I'm very disappointed.

Later in the evening, someone mentioned taking his kids to a trampoline party and then made a joke about the women's dodgy pelvic floors, as if vaginal leakage was an acceptable male conversation starter. But then several of the women in his circle laughed and affirmed his insight.

Fuck the lot of you, Ivy wanted to say. None of this is a fait accompli.

The usher really hit the spot with that madam, Ivy thinks.

But maybe I'm reading too much into it.

Maybe I'm overthinking.

Overthinking is a term that Ivy has thoroughly overthought. She dislikes it almost as much as madam.

But an accusation of overthinking is just what the usher might have said to Ivy. Don't overthink the madam thing, the young usher might have said. I was just being polite.

When I was her age, Ivy thinks, I was naive and egotistical. And then destroyed. Isn't it better to be in my forties? Isn't it better to be, as the phrase assumes one will be, both older and wiser? Yes. But. Yes. But. It still riles me.

Ivy can't stand the idea of someone young thinking of her as someone old, with all the judgments that go along with that. She remembers how she felt about older people when she was in her twenties. She had the indignant certainty of an educated young person edging into the adult world, assuming that all the best adults would share her clear-cut, black-and-white morality. She was disdainful toward the generation above her. She thought her love relationships would be more devoted than theirs, her

career would be more exceptional, her intoxications more dignified, her children better behaved, her politics less compromised,
her fashion less try-hard, her friendships more authentic. On it
went. But then things happened to Ivy, and she happened to
things, and the huge whirling gray of complex experience fogged
her crisp worldview, and humbled her.

She couldn't explain that transformation to Margot Pierce
over a five-minute chat at intermission. Perhaps it isn't even a
change that is noticeable to other people. Perhaps Ivy's young ar-
rogance wasn't too visible then, nor was her humility now. Perhaps she has transformed in secret ways that matter only to herself.

Ivy cringes to consider the person she was when she knew
Prof Pierce at university. She was an underprivileged student
with an extraordinary academic aptitude, who won scholarships
and prevailed, as though society were an ideal meritocracy and
she was the cream that rose to the top. She thought she was de-
serving of everything that came to her. She didn't think about
the poor kids who weren't unusually brainy. She didn't think
about collective fairness. She just thought about herself.

She was an orphan. She had suffered as a child, she had suffered as a teenager, and she would not suffer as an adult—it was
simple. She'd done her time, and she was ready to triumph. Ivy
was so sure about the quality of her future even though she had
no idea what it would entail.

She remembers asking Margot Pierce about what she should
pursue when she finished her degree.

You could do anything, Margot said.

You could do anything, is what everyone said to Ivy then.

The pink fizz. Winnie speaks.

The flute glasses.

The last guest gone.

Ivy thinks again of the usher in the foyer at the end of inter-mission. It wasn't just the madam that was off. It was something else. She didn't like the question about the art.

Ivy thought the girl was Indigenous. That's why she found her to ask about the paintings in the function room.

Ivy realizes now the layers of assumption that entails.

Why would the girl know or care about the art just because she was Aboriginal? And perhaps the girl isn't Indigenous at all. Did Ivy get that wrong? Did she out her somehow? Can a person be racially outed? Only if they are confused, or ashamed? Or in other circumstances too? Ivy is squirming at the thought.

As a teenager, Ivy unintentionally outed a gay boy at school who was being questioned about which of the girls in their class he had the hots for. He had neat sandy hair and round gold glasses, and he was very good at calculus. Ivy was sitting next to him on a beige leather couch at a house party, both of them drinking cans of syrupy premixed spirits. There were two or maybe three girls standing in front of the sofa, hands on hips, trying to be sassy, interrogating them about possible crushes.

You like boys, though, don't you? Ivy said to him, pulling her legs up under her, the soles of her sneakers squeaking the leather.

She remembers the look on his face, a wash of gratitude and fear.

He adjusted his glasses as his cheeks filled with blush. He tried to form a knowing grin. The girls burst into giggles and walked away.

Ivy hadn't meant to expose the boy. She just thought everyone saw what she saw.

Did the usher have a similar sweep of wary recognition across her face when Ivy asked her about the art?

The girl turned away from Ivy after deflecting the question, her long ponytail draping across the burgundy fabric of her uniform shirt. She shoved her hands into her trouser pockets and got on with whatever she needed to do. But before she turned, there was a moment when she may have noted, and despised, the presumption of the person standing beside her. Oh, here we go, she might have thought, here's the white woman assuming my heritage.

How awful, Ivy thinks. What a colonial fuckwit I am.

Or, alternatively, the usher is just having a bad night for reasons I do not understand, and her tone had nothing to do with me.

Don't overthink it, Ivy. Don't be so middle-aged.

Onstage, Willie has reappeared from behind Winnie's mound.

He is immaculately dressed in a morning suit and a black top hat as shiny as tree sap. A gold fob chain trails in a bright diagonal across his waistcoat. He is crawling on his hands and knees—his preferred mode of mobility—so that he resembles a member of a wedding party who has just dropped the bride's ring on the ground on his way to the church, his attempts at responsible formality undermined by the need to be peering closely at the earth.

But if Willie is looking for anything, he is looking for Winnie.

He is looking up the slope of the mound toward the beloved head at its peak.

He is crawling slowly and awkwardly up the mound toward her.

Well this is an unexpected pleasure! Reminds me of the day you came whining for my hand.

Winnie's stunned face is brightened by the sight of the man and, for the first time in a long time, she smiles a smile that is not mechanical.

Willie pauses in his endeavor and leans back against the dead slope he is climbing.

He might not reach Winnie's head after all. He might stop trying.

Sitting in the auditorium and looking down toward this scene, Ivy's eyes are drawn to Willie's gold watch chain, announcing its presence in the sun. It is glinting, brash and ridiculous in the harsh light of the stage. It seems affronting for there to be such a confident trinket in such a world.

Ivy once felt affronted by Prof Pierce's gold jewelry. She remembers an appointment she had in Margot's office that was so brief, Ivy did not even sit down. The professor did not stand up from behind her desk, not when Ivy walked in, and not to clear off the piles of splayed files from the only chair in the office that might have been available for Ivy to use. Instead, Ivy stood on a patch of dirty gray carpet, her bag on her shoulder, trying not to bump the stacks of newish books sticking out in front of the dense rows of older books filling the bookshelf wall.

The meeting was during a period when Ivy was running out of money each week, when she couldn't pick up enough shifts at work to loosen the financial vise that was forever throbbing across her chest. Her grandmother was fading and demanding, and completely dependent on her. Ivy was struggling to make it to class. She was convinced she was unable to complete her final assignments, all of them due within the same two days at the end of the semester. Ivy was grateful that Prof Pierce agreed to meet, so that she might be able to explain in person her need for an extension.

Margot was succinct with her advice, adept at churning through all the people making demands on her expertise, but Ivy was unable to listen to the few words she had to say. The professor was sitting at her desk, wearing a cluster of gold bangles on her wrists, and Ivy fixated on them. Each time Margot gesticulated, her hands rising up from behind the boxy desktop computer, her jewelry shook and shone on her arms.

Ivy got stuck feeling angry about those bangles, pondering the value of those bangles, and how any one of them could probably provide enough money for her to live off for a while. Each one—a few had colorful precious stones in them, another was a plait with three shades of intertwining gold—would be worth more than Ivy earned in a fortnight stirring through the buffet baked beans on the breakfast shift or delivering room service to semi-naked drunk men at the shitty three-star hotel where she worked. Ivy imagined that Margot never gave any thought to the value of her pointless, pretty trinkets. She'd just shove them onto her arms each morning and annoy people all day with the clanking, clinking assertion of them.

There are no bangles on Margot's wrists tonight, Ivy thinks. Only a watch with a thin black band.

Ivy presses her palms flat into her thighs below her skirt. Her wrists are also free of decorations. Ivy has never worn bracelets and maybe that's got something to do with the oblivious jewelry on Professor Pierce in the past. Ivy has not joined the dots on that before. It could be another small way that Margot influenced her.

If Ivy were to consider the most important people in her life, Professor Margot Pierce would be on that list. Maybe the memory of those bangles is so clear to Ivy because it is incongruous with her prevailing affection for Margot.

She always seemed bulletproof and perfect to Ivy—an impressive grown-up who had her impressive life under control, someone with a sense of purpose and ambition, and a supportive family she adored, to boot. Was there just the one child? Ivy thinks so. The son was an undergrad at a different university in a different discipline—lovingly avoiding his mother's shadow—at the same time that Ivy first appeared in Margot's orbit.

Margot was the first adult Ivy knew personally who she thought she might like to emulate. Someone real and not in a book. Margot was witty and stealthy. She had authority. Ivy's teachers at school and the mothers of her friends could not have been described in that way, not at all. And, then, as well as all the appeal of her own personal attributes, Margot Pierce responded to Ivy. She noticed her, saw her properly, so that Ivy, anchored by the recognition, could then get on with becoming herself.

Margot respected Ivy when she was a kid trying to be a sophisticate, when she was the student without the equipment-heavy hobbies and designer clothes of her peers, the girl who lived with her conservative, working-class grandmother in a suburb most of them had never heard of. Ivy was accustomed to that dynamic as the scholarship kid at school, and it was just as pronounced at uni. At school, Ivy's teachers were too intimidated by her disadvantage to encourage her further. They were just delighted to have her as part of the community! At university, Ivy remembers feeling that Professor Pierce listened to her ideas, thought that they were ideas, and thought that they were possibly even interesting ideas that could be challenged. Before Margot, Ivy had hardly encountered an adult who engaged with her much at all, except Hilary's parents.

Hilary had terrific parents. Her whole family was madcap and raucous and relentlessly conversational, and they all seemed to like each other so much. Her mother and father were forever taking group photographs and developing them and fitting them into the collage of images covering the walls in the separate toilet room in the family home. Ivy used to sit on their toilet—she spent so much time in that house—and look at the faces on both sides of her, and feel a yearning for such familial celebration and acceptance. She liked to imagine Hilary's mum selecting the images—This is a gorgeous shot of you, Hil. I love this one of us all. Doesn't your father look handsome here?—and then carefully cutting out the figures from the backgrounds and arranging them on the wall so that there was no space left around the heads. The walls were a crushing collection of human heads with very few bodies attached, and definitely no landscapes, backgrounds, birthday cakes, picnic rugs, dining tables. It was apparent that the family curatorial policy was to focus exclusively on the beloved faces, editing out the rest of the unnecessary world.

Ivy wonders if the next generation of Hilary's family have been layered over the original heads on the toilet wall. There are probably new images of Hilary's children pulling crazy children faces squashed alongside old photos of their mother as a teenager trying the vacant model poses of the '90s. Hilary went through a stage of only being photographed looking into the middle distance with her mouth a closed, ambiguous line. Is the photo of Hilary and Ivy at their school formal—the one Ivy felt so proud to have found in the face collage—still there on the wall? Or has it been replaced, supplanted by a wedding photo or a fresh baby? How many heads over how much time have been given a space on those walls?

The head on stage has plenty of space around her.

The head on stage is admiring Willie as he attempts to reach her.

Willie's neck is upturned and Winnie notices a mark on it. It is a red scab, an irregular shape. She is calling it an anthrax, and she is concerned.

Want to watch that, Willie, before it gets a hold on you.

What is the mark on Willie's neck meant to be telling us? Ivy wonders. What was SB getting at with that? She's never been sure.

Is it showing us that the man—apparently mobile and alive—is also dying incrementally and will soon be covered in a seething rash of toxicity? Is that it?

Or is it showing us that Willie's no more than an animal on all fours with an animal's disease? Is that it?

Or is it showing us that there's often an early indicator of what will become a far more significant problem? Is that it?

Ivy is concerned about Margot's bruises, and what they signify.

What are Margot's bruises telling the world?

They are of varying colors, varying shapes. They are unconcealed, yet inconclusive.

Ivy cannot settle on a viable theory about what is happening to Professor Pierce. Margot was shocked when Ivy asked her about the bruises, and her reply was an obvious lie. The bruises are not the result of a gardening accident. Margot is almost certainly not a gardener. How would she find the time to be a gardener? That was such a poor excuse, she may as well have just said, I ran into a door.

But what then? A health condition she doesn't want to talk

about? What kind of health condition leaves bruising all over the arms? A vitamin deficiency? Blood cancer? Ivy doesn't know.

Or is it possible someone could be hurting a woman like Margot? She's too formidable. She wouldn't accept being a victim of any kind, would she?

Ivy doesn't have any answers but she definitely wants them, and what she found most unsettling about her interaction with Margot at intermission was that they were being openly familiar with each other and then, suddenly, they were not. And the detail that is clear to Ivy—perhaps the only detail that is clear to Ivy—is that Margot's bruises are not a topic that Margot is used to discussing.

The professor made some other comments during intermission, about the bushfires. Margot complained about the extreme heat of the day and the smoke haze over the city. And the air conditioning. It gives me such a tickle in my throat, she said. And my eyes get terribly dry. She went into a lot of detail about the different eyedrops she has tried and how awful it is to have a cough at the theater. She denounced the auditorium air con for being set at a provocatively low temperature. I'm absolutely frigid in there, she said.

Ivy considers now that Margot complains about small issues because she is unable to complain about the real thing. It's a deflected quest for much-needed sympathy about something worse. In childbirth, Ivy focused on the minutiae of the hospital room—I need that curtain to be pushed aside! I need that pillow

placed right here! I need the bed raised a little! Not that much!—
instead of the agonizing waves of labor pain that left her incred-
ulous at the absurd brutality of the human experience. She could
have wailed about how much pain she was in but instead she
demanded adjustments to the furnishings. Yes, it is possible
Margot's complaints are a similar attempt to cope with what is
actually happening to her.

Look at me again, Willie, Winnie pleads. *Once more, Willie.*

On stage, Winnie is losing faith in her man's intentions. Is he
truly determined to reach her? He is making such slow progress
up the mound of dead earth that she is unsure if he will continue
the pursuit.

Is it me you're after, Willie . . . or is it something else?

Oh god, it might be the gun he craves.

Do you want to touch my face?

But then the man slides back off the slope completely, all
progress eliminated for now as he lies facedown on the hard, dry
ground, a hairbrush sticking out from beneath his leg, a music
box open and silent beside his ear.

There was a time, of course, when she could have given him
a hand.

There was a time, of course, when she could have reached a
long arm down toward him and hauled him up, forcing him to
face her, head to head.

But she only has her voice now to entice him.

Have another go, Willie, I'll cheer you on.

The play is nearing completion.

What a night this has been, Ivy thinks. Winnie's performance, but the people too, the unexpected encounters she will not leave behind.

Ivy used to hide in the ladies during events. She often had to attend functions as the recipient of a scholarship or the participant in some enrichment program, and she would dash out of the room as soon as the speeches ended to avoid any moment of the standing-around-and-speaking-to-people part of the party. She was unable to muster up enough self-assurance to trust that she could converse with strangers. The idea of chatting to people she did not know, who might ask her questions she did not want to answer, filled her with a nauseating dread.

But something shifted when she finished uni and moved overseas, and it was such a foreign experience that she was able to turn into whatever version of young-Australian-woman-abroad that was required. Her life didn't seem connected to reality enough to have any consequences. She learned to listen. She learned to notice. She learned to ask questions rather than waiting in fear to be asked them.

These days, she does not hide in bathrooms to avoid conversation. She isn't so afraid of herself or other people. She likes to think she can talk about anything—a carrot finger, a relationship that is unusually skewed, a philanthropic program. Ivy still overthinks the conversations she has, and worries about getting it wrong, and stuffs up occasionally—with the usher tonight, maybe with the professor too—but she is doing it.

She is not hiding. She has not given up.

Before the play began, Ivy didn't buy a souvenir program. There was a suave man selling them from on top of a stepped dais in the foyer.

Souvenir programs! he shouted theatrically across the busy space, holding up a copy of the booklet next to his cheek like a compact pet he was posing with for a photo.

Souvenir always struck Ivy as an excessive expectation for a theater program, especially one that might just contain some cast and crew photos and a brief biography of the playwright you could mostly find on Wikipedia. Maybe a single commissioned essay if the company was flush.

But I should get a souvenir program tonight, Ivy thinks. To mark my reunion with Margot Pierce, version 2.0 of our relationship. Once the play is over, I'll buy one in the foyer.

She could even prop the program open on her desk at the photo of Samuel Beckett and let herself love him again. What a mind he had to write these people on this earth. What a soul, indeed.

Win, the man says to Winnie. A single syllable.

And the audience adjusts in their seats, collectively.

Ivy feels the exaltation ripple through the theater—the sheer hopeful relief of that smallest utterance.

Win! Winnie smiles. *Oh this* is *a happy day . . .*

Willie is no longer prone on the flat ground. He is on his hands and knees again, staring up at Winnie from the base of the mound like a weary but determined animal. It appears he is once more going to attempt the ascent.

Winnie sings a love song.

> *Though I say not*
> *What I may not*
> *Let you hear,*

The play will finish with her song.

> *Every touch of fingers*
> *Tells me what I know,*

Beside Ivy, Daniel Glass is snoring. In a moment, during the applause, his sister will gently wake him.

> *It's true, it's true,*
> *You love me so!*

On stage, Winnie will bow to the audience from inside her mound, so her bow will be little more than a small nod of her head. Her expressive malleable face will present itself in the harsh light, exhausted.

When the lights darken to allow a surge in applause, Winnie will not climb out of her trap to appear whole again like a magician's assistant whose destruction was an illusion. Winnie will stay inside the mound. She will not appease the audience.

Willie will stand alongside Winnie's head, and also bow to the crowd.

A neat bend at the waist, hands clasped behind him like a butler.

Then Willie will take a step back—careful to avoid the garbage of Winnie's possessions strewn across the floor—and he will gesture toward the woman contained inside the stage.

He will smile a wide smile of admiration and humility, and clap his hands.

As the audience leaves the theater, Ivy will keep her eye on Professor Margot Pierce to ensure that she does not get too far away, so that they will not lose touch beyond this evening, so that the older woman might tell the younger one what is happening to her in her private life, and so that the younger woman might talk to the older one about her accumulated understanding of compromise and shame. Ivy will forget to buy a souvenir program.

Margot! Ivy will shout when she thinks the professor is moving too swiftly. Wait.

Margot will turn toward her name, and Ivy and Hilary will hurry through the crowd to catch up with her.

The women will walk together toward their parked cars.

And Ivy will notice the usher—the young usher—running from the theater building into the outside, holding a backpack and wearing her uniform, rushing into the hot, heavy air of the real world.

Thank You

To my constant friends and big loves—Katie Ridsdale and Annabelle Roxon.

To Laura Perciasepe, Alison Fairbrother, and the team at Riverhead.

To my Australian agent who remained interested in me when I was quiet, who told me her arms were open whenever I was ready—the extraordinarily steadfast and supportive Clare Forster of Curtis Brown.

To my American agent who was a delightful surprise—Noah Ballard of Curtis Brown.

To the other exemplary professionals who ensured a dream publishing experience—Robert Watkins, Fiona Hazard and the Hachette Australia team, Federico Andornino, Ali Lavau, Rebecca Allen, Bec Hamilton, Leah Jing McIntosh, and Alissa Dinallo.

To friends, family, and colleagues who supported me in many different ways for so long—Clare Bowditch, Patsy Brown, Sam Brown, Marion M. Campbell, Deirdre Coleman, Tyne Daile, Sasha Gattermayr, Makenna Goodman, Lisa Gorton, Andrea Hamilton, Samantha Howe, Joe Hughes, Martin Hughes, Angus Husband, James Jiang, Deidre D. Johnson, Coralie Kane, Domini Marshall, Anne Maxwell, Rachel Mudge, Lara

Stevens, Charlotte Wood, treasured writerly confidante Emily Bitto, and my beloved parents, Cheryl and Chris Thomas.

To life-affirming facilitators—Andrea Dupree and all at the Lighthouse Writers Workshop in Denver, Colorado, especially Sheila Heti and Leslie Jamison, who are the writers I needed to find.

To comrades of the Casual Network of the University of Melbourne NTEU for being a beacon of positive activism, particularly Ben Kunkler and Nick Robinson.

To the staff and creative community at the Abbotsford Convent, Melbourne.

To the Australia Council for the Arts and the trustees of the Felix Meyer Scholarship.

To the creators of resonant artworks—French & Mottershead (*Bushland* in Chapter 5) and Cornelia Parker (*Embryo Firearms* in Chapter 6).

To my students, particularly my supervisees and those from Literature, Ecology, Catastrophe, who enlivened, challenged, and inspired me.

To my devoted story listener, who always wanted more—Andrew Young.

To my big children for believing I was a writer when I wasn't writing, and for being so proud and excited when I did it—Camille and Leonard.

To my small child for bringing abundant life joy—Angus.

This novel was written, with gratitude, admiration, and respect, on the land of the Wurundjeri People of the Kulin Nation.

Always was, always will be, Aboriginal land.